THE NATURE OF A CRIME

Robert Hampson is Professor of Modern Literature at Royal Holloway, University of London. He is the author of *Joseph Conrad: Betrayal and Identity*, *Cross-Cultural Encounters in Joseph Conrad's Malay Fiction* and *Conrad's Secrets*; co-editor of *Conrad and Theory*, *Ford Madox Ford: A Reappraisal* and *Ford Madox Ford and Modernity*; and editor of various works by Conrad (including *Heart of Darkness, Lord Jim, Victory*, and *Nostromo*), Kipling (including *Something of Myself, Soldiers Three* and *In Black & White*) and Rider Haggard (*King Solomon's Mines*).

THE NATURE OF A CRIME

BY
Joseph Conrad
AND
Ford Madox Ford

ReScript Books

RESCRIPT BOOKS is an imprint of
REALITY STREET
63 All Saints Street, Hastings TN34 3BN
www.realitystreet.co.uk/rescript-books.php

First published 1924
First ReScript Books edition, 2012

A catalogue record for this book is available from the British Library

ISBN: 978-1-874400-60-8

CONTENTS

PREFACE
By Joseph Conrad

FOR years my consciousness of this small piece of collaboration has been very vague, almost impalpable, like the
fleeting visits from a ghost. If I ever thought of it, and I
must confess that I can hardly remember ever doing it on
purpose till it was brought definitely to my notice by my
collaborator, I always regarded it as something in the
nature of a fragment. I was surprised and even shocked
to discover that it was rounded. But I need not have been.
Rounded as it is in form, using the word form in its sim-
plest sense—printed form—it remains yet a fragment
from its very nature and also from necessity. It could
never have become anything else. And even as a fragment
it is but a fragment of something that might have been—
of a mere intention.

But as it stands what impresses me most is the amount
this fragment contains of the crudely materialistic atmosphere of the time of its origin, the time when the *English
Review* was founded. It emerges from the depth of a past
as distant from us now as the square-skirted, long frock-
coats in which unscrupulous, cultivated, high-minded
jouisseurs like ours here attended to their strange business

7

activities and cultivated the little blue flower of sentiment. No doubt our man was conceived for purposes of irony; but our conception of him, I fear, is too fantastic.

Yet the most fantastic thing of all, as it seems to me, is that we two, who had so often discussed soberly the limits and the methods of literary composition, should have believed, for a moment, that a piece of work in the nature of an analytical confession (produced *in articulo mortis* as it were) could have been developed and achieved in collaboration!

What optimism! But it did not last long. I seem to remember a moment when I burst into earnest entreaties that all those people should be thrown overboard without much ado. This, I believe, *is* the real nature of the crime. Overboard. The neatness and dispatch with which it is done in Chapter VIII were wholly the act of my collaborator's good nature in the face of my panic.

After signing these few prefatory words, I will pass the pen to him in the hope that he may be moved to contradict me on every point of fact, impression and appreciation. I said " the hope." Yes. Eager hope. For it would be delightful to catch the echo of the desperate, earnest, eloquent and funny quarrels which enlivened those old days. The pity of it that there comes a time when all the fun of one's life must be looked for in the past!

J. C.

June 1924

PREFACE
By Ford Madox Ford

No, I find nothing to contradict, for, the existence of this story having been recalled to my mind by a friend, the details of its birth and its attendant circumstances remain for me completely forgotten, a dark, blind spot on the brain. I cannot remember the houses in which the writing took place, the view from the windows, the pen, the table-cloth. At a given point in my life I forgot, literally, all the books I had ever written; but, if nowadays I reread one of them, though I possess next to none and have reread few, nearly all the phrases come back startlingly to my memory, and I see glimpses of Kent, of Sussex, of Carcassonne—of New York, even; and fragments of furniture, mirrors, who knows what? So that, if I didn't happen to retain, almost by a miracle, for me, of retention, the marked up copy of *Romance* from which was made the analysis lately published in a certain periodical, I am certain that I could have identified the phrases exactly as they stand. Looking at the book now I can hear our voices as we read one passage or another aloud for purposes of correction. Moreover, I could say: This passage was written in Kent and hammered over in Sussex; this, written in Sussex and worked on in Kent; or this again was written in the downstairs café, and hammered in the sitting-room on the first-floor of an hotel that faces the sea on the Belgian coast.

But of the *Nature of a Crime* no phrase at all suggests either the tones of a voice or the colour of a day. When an old friend, last year, on a Parisian Boulevard, said: "Isn't there a story by yourself and Collaborator buried in the So and So?" I repudiated the idea with a great deal of heat. Eventually I had to admit the, as it were, dead fact. And. having admitted that to myself, and my Collaborator having corroborated it, I was at once possessed by a sort of morbid craving to get the story republished in a definite and acknowledged form. One may care infinitely little for the fate of one's work, and yet be almost hypochondriacally anxious as to the form its publication shall take—if the publication is likely to occur posthumously. I became at once dreadfully afraid that some philologist of that Posterity for which one writes might, in the course of his hyena occupation, disinter these poor bones, and, attributing sentence one to writer A and sentence two to B, maul at least one of our memories. With the nature of *those* crimes one is only too well acquainted. Besides, though one may never read comments one desires to get them over. It is, indeed, agreeable to hear a storm rage in the distance, and rumble eventually away.

Let me, however, since my Collaborator wishes it, and in the name of Fun that is to-day hardly an echo, differ from him for a shade as to the nature of those passages of time. I protest against the word quarrels. There were not any. And I should like to make the note that our collaboration was almost purely oral. We wrote and read aloud the one to the other. Possibly in the end we even wrote *to* read aloud the one to the other: for it strikes me very forcibly that the *Nature of a Crime* is for the most part prose meant for recitation, or of that type.

Anyhow, as the memory comes back to me overwhelmingly, I would read on and read on. One begins with a fine propulsion. Sometimes that would last to the end. But, as often as not, by a real telepathy, with my eyes on the page and my voice going on, I would grow aware of an exaggerated stillness on the part of my Collaborator in the shadows. It was an extraordinary kind of stillness: not of death: not of an ice age. Yes, it was the stillness of a prisoner on the rack determined to conceal an agony. I would read on, my voice gradually sticking to my jaws. When it became unbearable I would glance up. On the other side of the hearth I would have a glimpse of a terribly sick man, of a convulsed face, of fingers contorted. Guido Fawkes beneath the *peine forte et dure* looked like that. You are to remember that we were very serious about writing. I would read on. After a long time it would come: "Oh! ... Oh, Oh! ... Oh, my God.... My dear Ford.... My dear faller...." (That in those days was the fashionable pronunciation of " fellow.")

For myself, I would listen always with admiration. Always with an admiration that I have never since recaptured. And if there were admirablenesses that did not seem to me to fit in with the given scene, I could at least, at the end of the reading, say with perfect sincerity: "Wonderful! *How* you do things! ..." before beginning on: "But don't you perhaps think...."

And I really do not believe that either my Collaborator or myself ever made an objection, which was not jointly sustained. That is not quarrels. When I last looked through the bound proofs of *Romance* I was struck with the fact that whereas my Collaborator eliminated almost every word of action and 80 per cent. of the conversations by myself, I supplied almost all the descriptive passages of the really collaborated parts—and such softer sentiment as was called for. And my Collaborator let them get through.

All this took place long ago; most of it in another century, during another reign; whilst an earlier, but not less haughty and proud, generation were passing away.

F.M.H.

June 1924

THE NATURE OF A CRIME

I

YOU are, I suppose, by now in Rome. It is very curious how present to me are both Rome and yourself. There is a certain hill—you, and that is the curious part of it, will never go there—yet, yesterday, late in the evening, I stood upon its summit, and you came walking from a place below. It is always midday there: the seven pillars of the Forum stand on high, their capitals linked together, and form one angle of a square. At their bases there lie some detritus, a broken marble lion, and I think but I am not certain, the bronze she-wolf suckling the two bronze children. Your dress brushed the herbs: it was grey and tenuous: I suppose you do not know how you look when you are unconscious of being looked at? But I looked at you for a long time—at my You.

I saw your husband yesterday at the club and he said that you would not be returning till the end of April. When I got back to my chambers I found a certain letter. I will tell you about it afterwards—but I forbid you to look at the end of what I am writing now. There is a piece of news coming: I would break it to you if I could—but

13

there is no way of breaking the utterly unexpected. Only, if you read this through you will gather from the tenor, from the tone of my thoughts, a little inkling, a small preparation for my disclosure. Yes: it is a "disclosure."

... Briefly, then, it was this letter—a business letter— that set me thinking: that made that hill rise before me. Yes, I stood upon it and there before me lay Rome— beneath a haze, in the immense sea of plains. I have often thought of going to Rome—of going with you, in a leisurely autumn of your life and mine. Now—since I have received that letter—I know that I shall never see any other Rome than that from an imagined hilltop. And when, in the wonderful light and shadelessness of that noon, last evening, you came from a grove of silver poplars, I looked at you—*my* you—for a very long while. You had, I think, a parasol behind your head, you moved slowly, you looked up at the capitals of those seven pillars ... And I thought that I should never—since you will not return before the end of April—never see you again. I shall never see again the you that every other man sees ...

You understand everything so well that already you must understand the nature of my disclosure. It is, of course, no disclosure to tell you that I love you. A very great reverence is due to youth—and a very great latitude is due to the dead. For I am dead: I have only lived through you for how many years now ! And I shall never speak with you again. Some sort of burial will have been given to me before the end of April. I am a spirit. I have ended my relations with the world. I have balanced all my books, my will is made. Only I have nothing to leave—save to you, to whom I leave all that is now mine in the world—my memory.

It is very curious—the world now. I walked slowly down here from Gordon Square. I walked slowly—for all my work is done. On the way I met Graydon Bankes, the K.C. It would have astonished him if he could have known how unreal he looked to me. He is six feet high, and upon his left cheek there is a brown mole. I found it difficult to imagine why he existed. And all sorts of mists hurried past him. It was just outside the Natural History Museum. He said that his Seaford Railway Bill would come before Committee in June. And I wondered: what is June? ... I laughed and thought: why June will never come!

June will never come. Imagine that for a moment. We have discussed the ethics of suicide. You see why June will never come!

You remember that ring I always wear? The one with a bulging, greenish stone. Once or twice you have asked me what stone it was. You thought, I know, that it was in bad taste and I told you I wore it for the sake of associations. I know you thought—but no: there has never been any woman but you.

You must have felt a long time ago that there was not, that there could not have been another woman. The associations of the ring are not with the past of a finished affection, or hate, or passion, to all these forms of unrest that have a term in life: they looked forward to where there is no end—whether there is rest in it God alone knows. If it were not bad taste to use big words in extremities I would say there was Eternity in the ring— Eternity which is the negation of all that life may contain of losses and disappointments. Perhaps you have noticed that there was one note in our confidence that never responded to your touch. It was that note of universal negation contained within the glass film of the ring. It is not you who brought the ring into my life: I had it made years ago. It was in my nature always to anticipate a touch on my shoulder, to which the only answer could be an act of defiance. And the ring is my weapon. I shall raise it to my teeth, bite through the glass: inside there is poison.

I haven't concealed anything from you. Have I? And, with the great wisdom for which I love you, you have tolerated these other things. You would have tolerated this too, you who have met so many sinners and have never sinned ...

Ah, my dear one—that is why I have so loved you. From our two poles we have met upon one common ground of scepticism—so that I am not certain whether it was you or I who first said: "Believe nothing: be harsh to no one." But at least we have suffered. One does not drag around with one such a cannon-ball as I have done all these years without thinking some wise thoughts. And well I know that in your dreary and terrible life you have gained your great wisdom. You have been envied; you too have thought: Is any prospect fair to those among its trees? And I have been envied for my gifts, for my talents, for my wealth, for my official position, for the letters after my name, for my great and empty house, for my taste in pictures—for my ... for my opportunities.

Great criminals and the very patient learn one common lesson: Believe in nothing, be harsh to no one!

But you cannot understand how immensely leisurely I feel. It is one o'clock at night. I cannot possibly be arrested before eleven to-morrow morning. I have ten hours in which, without the shadow of a doubt, I can write to you: I can put down my thoughts desultorily and lazily. I have half a score hours in which to speak to you.

The stress of every secret emotion makes for sincerity in the end. Silence is like a dam. When the flood is at its highest the dam gives way. I am not conceited enough to think that I can sweep you along, terrified, in the rush of my confidences. I have not the elemental force. Perhaps it is just that form of "greatness" that I have lacked all my life—that profound quality which the Italians call *terribilità*. There is nothing overpowering or terrible in the confession of a love too great to be kept within the bounds of the banality which is the safeguard of our daily life. Men have been nerved to crime for the sake of a love that was theirs. The call of every great passion is to unlawfulness. But your love was not mine, and my love for you was vitiated by that conventional reverence which, as to nine parts in ten, is genuine, but as to the last tenth a solemn sham behind which hide all the timidities of a humanity no longer in its youth. I have been of my time—altogether of my time—lacking courage for a swoop, as a bird respects a ragged and nerveless scarecrow. Altogether a man of my time. Observe, I do not say "our time." You are of all time—you are the loved Woman of the first cry that broke the silence and of the last song that shall mark the end of this ingenious world to which love and suffering have been given, but which has in the course of ages invented for itself all the virtues and all the crimes. And being of this world and of my time I have set myself to deal ingeniously with my suffering and my love.

Now everything is over—even regrets. Nothing remains of finite things but a few days of life and my confession to make to you—to you alone of all the world.

It is difficult. How am I to begin? Would you believe it —every time I left your presence it was with the desire, with the necessity to forget you. Would you believe it?

This is the great secret—the heart of my confession. The distance did not count. No walls could make me safe. No solitude could defend me; and having no faith in the consolations of eternity I suffered too cruelly from your absence.

If there had been kingdoms to conquer, a crusade to preach—but no. I should not have had the courage to go beyond the sound of your voice. You might have called to me any time! You never did. Never. And now it is too late.

Moreover, I am a man of my time, the time is not of great deeds but of colossal speculations. The moments when I was not with you had to be got through somehow. I dared not face them empty-handed lest from sheer distress I should go mad and begin to execrate you. Action? What form of action could remove me far enough from you whose every thought was referred to your existence. And as you were to me a soul of truth and serenity I tried to forget you in lies and excitement. My only refuge from the tyranny of my desire was in abasement. Perhaps I was mad. I gambled. I gambled first with my own money and then with money that was not mine. You know my connection with the great Burden fortune. I was trustee under my friend's, Alexander Burden's will. I gambled with a determined recklessness, with closed eyes. You understand now the origin of my houses, of my collections, of my reputation, of my taste for magnificence—which you deigned sometimes to mock indulgently with an exquisite flattery as at something not quite worthy of me. It was like a break-neck ride on a wild horse, and now the fall has come. It was sudden. I am alive but my back is broken. Edward Burden is going to be married. I must pay back what I have borrowed from the Trust. I cannot. Therefore I am dead. (A mouse has just come out from beneath one of the deed-boxes. It looks up at me. It may have been eating some of the papers in the large cupboard. To-morrow morning I shall tell Saunders to get a cat. I have never seen a mouse here before. I have never been here so late before. At times of pressure, as you know, I have always taken my papers home. So that these late hours have been, as it were, the prerogative of the mouse. No. I shall not get a cat. To that extent I am still a part of the world: I am master of the fate of mice!) I have, then, ten hours, less the time it has taken me to chronicle the mouse, in which to talk to you. It is strange, when I look back on it, that in all the years we have known each other—seven years, three months and two days—I have never had so long as ten hours in which I might talk to you. The longest time was when we came back from Paris together, when your husband was in such a state that he could neither see nor hear. (I've seen him, by-the-bye, every day since you have been gone. He's really keeping away from it wonderfully well; in fact, I should say that he has not once actually succumbed. I fancy, really, that your absence is good for him in a way: it creates a new set of circumstances, and a change is said to be an excellent aid in the breaking of a habit. He has, I mean, to occupy himself with some of the things, innumerable as they are, that you do for him. I find that he has even had his pass-book from the bank and has compared it with his counter-foils. I haven't, on account of this improvement, yet been round to his chemist's. But I shall certainly tell them that they *must* surreptitiously decrease the strength of it.) That was the longest time we have ever really talked together. And, when I think that in all these years I haven't once so much as held your hand for a moment longer than the strictest of etiquette demanded! And I loved you within the first month.

I wonder why that is. Fancy, perhaps. Habit perhaps— a kind of idealism, a kind of delicacy, a fastidiousness. As you know very well it is not on account of any moral scruples....

I break off to look through what I have already written to you. There is, first, the question of why I never told you my secret: then, the question of what my secret really is; I have started so many questions and have not followed one of them out to the very end. But all questions resolve themselves into the one question of our dear and inestimable relationship.

I think it has been one of the great charms of our relationship that all our talks have been just talks. We have discussed everything under the sun, but we have never discussed anything *au fond*. We have strayed into all sorts of byways and have never got anywhere. I try to remember how many evenings in the last five years we have not spent together. I think they must be less than a hundred in number. You know how, occasionally, your husband would wake out of his stupors—or walk *in* his stupor and deliver one of his astonishingly brilliant disquisitions. But remember how, always, whether he talked of free love or the improvement in the breed of carriage-horses, how he always thrashed his subject out to the bitter end. It was not living with a man: it was assisting at a performance. And, when he was sunk into his drugs or when he was

21

merely literary, or when he was away, how lazily we talked. I think no two minds were ever so fitted one into another as yours and mine. It is not of course that we agree on all subjects—or perhaps upon any. In the whole matter of conduct we are so absolutely different—you are always for circumspection, for a careful preparation of the ground, for patience; and I am always ready to act, and afterwards draw the moral from my own actions. But somehow, in the end, it has all worked out in our being in perfect agreement. Later I will tell you why that is.

Let me return to my mouse. For you will observe that the whole question revolves, really, around that little allegorical mite. It is an omen: it is a symbol. It is a little herald of the Providence that I do not believe in—of the Providence you so implicitly seek to obey. For instinctively you believe in Providence—in God, if you will. I as instinctively disbelieve. Intellectually of course you disbelieve in a God. You say that it is impossible for Reason to accept an Overlord; I that Reason forces one to accept an Overlord; I that Reason forces one to believe in an Omnipotent Ruler—only I am unable to believe. We, my dear, are in ourselves evidence of a design in creation. For we are the last word of creation. It has taken all the efforts, all the birthpangs of all the ages to evolve—you and me. And, being evolved, we are intellectually so perfectly and so divinely fashioned to dovetail together. And, physically too, are we not divinely meant the one for the other? Do we not react to the same causes: should not we survive the same hardships or succumb to the same stresses? Since you have been away I have gone looking for people—men, women, children, even animals—that could hold my attention for a minute. There has not been one. And what purer evidence of design could you ask for than that?

I have made this pact with the Providence that I argue for, with the Providence in whose existence I cannot believe—that if, from under the castle of black metal boxes, the mouse reappear and challenge death—then there is no future state. And, since I can find no expression save in you, if we are not reunited I shall no longer exist. So my mouse is the sign, the arbitrament, a symbol of an eternal life or the herald of nothingness.

I will make to you the confession that since this fancy, this profound truth, has entered my mind, I have not raised my eyes from the paper. I dread—I suppose it is dread—to look across the ring of light that my lamp casts. But now I will do so. I will let my eyes travel across the bundles of dusty papers on my desk. Do you know I have left them just as they were on the day when you came to ask me to take your railway tickets? I will let my eyes travel across that rampart of blue and white dockets.... The mouse is not there.

But that is not an end of it. I am not a man to be ungenerous in my dealings with the Omnipotent: I snatch no verdict.

II

LAST night it was very late and I grew tired, so I broke off my letter. Perhaps I was really afraid of seeing that mouse again. Those minute superstitions are curious things. I noticed, when I looked at the enumeration of these pages to-night, I began to write upon the thirteenth sheet—and that gives me a vague dissatisfaction. I read, by-the-bye, a paragraph in a newspaper: it dealt with half-mad authors. One of these, the writer said, was Zola; he was stated to be half-mad because he added together the numbers on the backs of cabs passing him in the street. Personally, I do that again and again—and I know very well that I do it in order to dull my mind. It is a sort of narcotic. Johnson, we know, touched his street-posts in a certain order: that, too, was to escape from miserable thoughts. And we all know how, as children, we have obeyed mysterious promptings to step upon the lines between the paving-stones in the street.... But the children have their futures: it is well that they should propitiate the mysterious Omnipotent One. In their day, too, Johnson and Zola had their futures. It was well that Johnson should "touch" against the evil chance; that Zola should rest his mind against new problems. In me it is mere imbecility. For I have no future.

24

Do you find it difficult to believe that? You know the Burdens, of course. But I think you do not know that, for the last nine years, I have administered the Burden estates all by myself. The original trustees were old Lady Burden and I; but nine years ago Lady Burden gave me a power of attorney and since then I have acted alone. It was just before then that I had bought the houses in Gordon Square—the one I live in, the one you live in, and the seven others. Well, rightly speaking, those houses have been bought with Burden money, and all my pictures, all my prints, all my books, my furniture—my reputation as a connoisseur, my governorship of the two charities—all the me that people envy have been bought with the Burden money. I assure you that at times I have found it a pleasurable excitement.... You see, I have wanted you sometimes so terribly—so terribly that the juggling with the Burden accounts has been as engrossing a narcotic as to Zola was the adding up of the numbers upon the backs of cabs. Mere ordinary work would never have held my thoughts.

Under old Burden's will young Edward Burden comes of age when he reaches the age of twenty-five or when he marries with my consent. Well, he will reach the age of twenty-five and he will marry on April 5. On that day the solicitors of his future wife will make their scrutiny of my accounts. It is regarded, you understand, as a mere formality. But it amuses me to think of the faces of Coke and Coke when they come to certain figures! It was an outlaw of some sort, was it not, who danced and sang beneath the gallows? I wonder, now, what sort of traitor, outlaw, or stealthy politician I should have made in the Middle Ages. It is certain that, save for this one particular of property, I should be in very truth illustrious. No doubt the state shall come at last in which there shall no more be any property. I was born before my time.

For it is certain that I am illustrious save in that one respect. To-day young Edward Burden came here to the office to introduce me to his *fiancée*. You observe that I have robbed her. The Burden property is really crippled. They came, this bright young couple, to get a cheque from me with which to purchase a motor-car. They are to try several cars in the next three weeks. On the day before the wedding they are to choose one that will suit them best—and on the wedding-day in the evening they are to start for Italy. They will be coming towards you.... Then no doubt, too, a telegram will reach them, to say that in all probability motor-cars will be things not for them for several years to come. What a crumbling of their lives!

It was odd how I felt towards *her*. You know his pompous, high forehead, the shine all over him, the grave, weighty manner. He held his hat—a wonderful shiny, "good" hat—before his mouth, for all the world as if he had been in church. He made, even, a speech in introducing Miss Averies to me. You see, in a sense, he was in a temple. My office enshrined a deity, a divinity: the law, property, the rights of man as maintained by an august constitution. I am for him such a wonderfully "safe" man. My dear one, you cannot imagine how I feel towards him: a little like a deity, a little like an avenging Providence. I imagine that the real Deity must feel towards some of His worshippers much as I feel towards this phoenix of the divines.

The Deity is after all the supreme Artist—and the supreme quality of Art is surprise.

Imagine then the feeling of the Deity towards some of those who most confidently enter His temple. Just imagine His attitude towards those who deal in the obvious platitudes that "honesty is the best policy," or "genius the capacity for taking pains." So for days the world appears to them. Then suddenly: honesty no longer pays; the creature, amassing with his infinite pains, data for his Great Work, is discovered to have produced a work of an Infinite Dulness. That is the all-suffering Deity manifesting Himself to His worshippers. For assuredly a day comes when two added to two no longer results in four. That day will come on April 5 for Edward Burden.

After all he has done nothing to make two and two become four. He has not even checked his accounts. Well, for some years now I have been doing as much as that. But with his *fiancée* it is different. She is a fair, slight girl with eyes that dilate under all sorts of emotion. In my office she appears not a confident worshipper but a rather frightened fawn led before an Anthropomorphic Deity. And, strangely enough, though young Burden who trusts me inspires me with a sardonic dislike, I felt myself saying to this poor little thing that faced me: "Why: I have wronged you!" And I regretted it.

She, you see, has after all given something towards a right to enjoy the Burden estates and the Burden wealth; she has given her fragile beauty, her amiability, her worship, no doubt, of the intolerable Edward. And all this payment in the proper coin; so she has in a sense a right....

Good-night, dear one, I think you have it in your power—you *might* have it in your power—to atone to this little creature. To-morrow I will tell you why and how.

III

I WROTE last night that you have something in your power. If you wished it you could make me live on. I am confident that you will not wish it: for you will understand that capriciously or intolerably I am tired of living this life. I desire you so terribly that now, even the excitement of fooling Burden no longer hypnotises me into an acceptance of life without you. Frankly, I am tired out. If I had to go on living any longer I should have to ask you to be mine in one form or other. With that and with my ability—for of course I have great ability—I could go on fooling Burden for ever. I could restore: I could make sounder than ever it was that preposterous "going concern" the Burden Estate. Unless I like to let them, I think that the wife's solicitors will not discover what I have done. For, frankly, I have put myself out in this matter in order to be amusing to myself and ingenious. I have forged whole builder's estimates for repairs that were never executed: I have invented whole hosts of defaulting tenants. It has not been latterly for money that I have done this: it has been simply for the sheer amusement of looking at Edward Burden and saying to myself:

"Ah: you trust me, my sleek friend. Well...."

But indeed I fancy that I am rich enough to be able to restore to them all that I have taken. And, looking at Edward Burden's little *fiancée*, I was almost tempted to set upon that weary course of juggling. But I am at the end of my tether. I cannot live without you longer. And I do not wish to ask you. Later I will tell you. Or No—I will tell you now.

You see, my dear thing, it is a question of going one better. It would be easy enough to deceive your husband: it would be easier still to go away together. I think that neither you nor I have ever had any conscientious scruples. But, analysing the matter down to its very depths, I think we arrive at this, that without the motives for self-restraint that other people have we are anxious to show more self-restraint than they. We are doing certain work not for payment but for sheer love of work. Do I make myself clear? For myself I have a great pride in your image. I can say to myself: "Here is a woman, my complement. She has no respect for the law. She does not value what a respect for the law would bring her. Yet she remains purer than the purest of the makers of law." And I think it is the converse of that feeling that you have for me.

If you desire me to live on, I will live on: I am so swayed by you that if you desire me to break away from this ideal of you, the breath of a command will send me round to your side.

I am ready to give my life for this Ideal: nay more, I am ready to sacrifice you to it, since I know that life for you will remain a very bitter thing. I know, a little, what renunciation means.

And I am asking you to bear it—for the sake of my ideal of you. For, assuredly, unless I can have you I must die—and I know that you will not ask me to have you. And I love you: and bless you for it.

IV

I HAVE just come in from *Tristan and Isolde.*

I had to hurry and be there for the first notes because you—my you—would, I felt, be sitting beside me as you have so often. That, of course, is passion—the passion that makes us unaccountable in our actions.

I found you naturally: but I found, too, something else. It has always a little puzzled me why we return to Tristan. There are passages in that thing as intolerable as anything in any of the Germanic master's scores. But we are held—simply by the idea of the love-philtre: it's that alone that interests us. We do not care about the initial amenities of Tristan and the prima donna: we do not believe in Mark's psychologising: but, from the moment when those two dismal marionettes have drained unconsideringly the impossible cup, they become suddenly alive, and we see two human beings under the grip of a passion—acting as irrationally as I did when I promised my cabman five shillings to get me to the theatre in time for the opening bars.

It is, you see, the love-philtre that performs this miracle. It interests—it is real to us—because every human being knows what it is to act, irrationally, under the stress of some passion or other. We are drawn along irresistibly: we commit the predestined follies or the predestined heroisms: the other side of our being acts in contravention of all our rules of conduct or of intellect. Here, in Tristan, we see such madness justified with a concrete substance, a herb, a root. We see a vision of a state of mind in which morality no longer exists: we are given a respite, a rest: an interval in which no standard of conduct oppresses us. It is an idea of an appeal more universal than any other in which the tired imagination of humanity takes refuge.

The thought that somewhere in the world there should be something that I could give to you, or you to me, that would leave us free to do what we wish without the drag of the thought of what we owe, to each other, to the world! And after all, what greater gift could one give to another? It would be the essential freedom. For assuredly, the philtre could do no more than put it in a man's power to do what he would do if he were let loose. He would not bring out more than he had in him: but he would fully and finally express himself.

Something unexpected has changed the current of my thoughts. Nothing can change their complexion, which is governed not by what others do but by the action which I must face presently. And I don't know why I should use the word unexpected, unless because at the moment I was very far from expecting that sort of perplexity. The correct thing to say would be that something natural has happened.

Perfectly natural. Asceticism is the last thing that one could expect from the Burdens. Alexander Burden, the father, was an exuberant millionaire, in no vulgar way, of course; he was exuberant with restraint, not for show, with a magnificence which was for private satisfaction mainly. I am talking here of the ascetic temperament which is based on renunciation, not of mere simplicity of tastes, which is simply scorn for certain orders of sensations. There have been millionaires who have lived simply. There have been millionaires who have lived sordidly—but miserliness is one of the supreme forms of sensualism.

Poor Burden had a magnificent physique. The reserved abilities of generations of impoverished Burdens, starved for want of opportunities, matured in his immense success—and all their starved appetites too. But all the reserve quality of obscure Burdens has been exhausted in him. There was nothing to come to his son—who at most could have been a great match and is to-day looked upon in that light, I suppose, by the relations of his future wife. I don't know in what light that young man looks upon himself. His time of trial is coming.

Yesterday at eight in the evening he came to see me. I thought at first he wanted some money urgently. But very soon I reflected that he need not have looked so embarrassed in that case. And presently I discovered that it was not money that he was in need of. He looked as though he had come, with that characteristic gravity of his—so unlike his father—to seek absolution at my hands. But that intention he judged more decorous, I suppose, to present to me as a case of conscience.

Of course it was the case of a girl—not his *fiancée*. At first I thought he was in an ugly scrape. Nothing of the kind. The excellent creature who had accepted his protection for some two years past—how dull they must have seemed to her—was perhaps for that reason perfectly resigned to forgo that advantage. At the same time, she was not too proud to accept a certain provision, compensation—whatever you like to call it. I had never heard of anything so proper in my life. He need not have explained the matter to me at all. But evidently he had made up his mind to indulge in the luxury of a conscience.

To indulge that sort of conscience leads one almost as far as indulged passion, only, I cannot help thinking, on a more sordid road. A luxury snatched from the fire is in a way purified, but to find this one he had gone apparently to the bottom of his heart. I don't charge him with a particularly odious degree of corruption, but I perceived clearly that what he wanted really was to project the sinful effect of that irregular connection—let us call it—into his regulated, reformed, I may say lawfully blessed state—for the sake of retrospective enjoyment, I suppose. This rather subtle, if unholy, appetite, he was pleased to call the voice of his conscience. I listened to his dialectic exercises till the great word that was sure to come out sooner or later was pronounced.

"It seems," he said, with every appearance of distress,

"that from a strictly moral point of view I ought to make a clean breast of it to Annie."

I listened to him—and, by Heaven, listening to him I *do* feel like the Godhead of whom I have already written to you. You know, positively he said that at the very moment of his "fall" he had thought of what *I* should think of him. And I said:

"My good Edward, you are the most debauched person I have ever met."

His face fell, his soft lips dropped right down into a horseshoe. He had come to me as one of those bland optimists *would* go to his deity. He expected to be able to say: "I have sinned," and to be able to hear the deity say: "That's all right, your very frank confession does you infinite credit." His deity was, in fact, to find him some way out of his moral hole. I was to find him some genial excuse; to make him feel good in his excellent digestion once more. That was, absolutely, his point of view, for at my brutal pronouncement he stuttered:

"But—but surely ... the faults of youth ... and surely there are plenty of others? ..."

I shook my head at him and panic was dropping out of his eyes: "Can't I marry Annie honourably?" he quavered. I took a sinister delight in turning the knife inside him. I was going to let him go anyhow: the sort of cat that I am always lets its mice go. (That mouse, by-the-bye, has never again put in an appearance.)

"My dear fellow," I said, "does not your delicacy let

you see the hole you put me into? It's to my interest that you should not marry Miss Averies and you ask me to advise you on the point."

His mouth dropped open: positively he had never considered that when he married I lost the confounded three hundred a year for administering the Burden Trust. I sat and smiled at him to give him plenty of time to let his mind agonise over his position.

"Oh, hang it," he said.... And his silly eyes rolled round my room looking for that Providence that he felt ought to intervene in his behalf. When they rested on me again I said:

"There, go away. Of course it's a fault of your youth. Of course every man that's fit to call himself a man has seduced a clergyman's daughter."

He said :

"Oh, but there was not anything common about it."

"No," I answered, "you had an uncommonly good time of it with your moral scruples. I envy you the capacity. You'll have a duller one with Miss Averies, you know."

That was too much for him to take in, so he smoothed his hat.

"When you said I was ... debauched ... you were only laughing at me. That was hardly fair. I'm tremendously in earnest."

"You're only play-acting compared with me," I answered. He had the air of buttoning his coat after putting a cheque into his breast pocket. He had got, you see, the cheque he expected: my applause of his successful seduction, my envy of his good fortune. That was what he had come for—and he got it. He went away with it pretty barefacedly, but he stopped at the threshold to let drop:

"Of course if I had known you would be offended by my having recourse to Annie's solicitors for the settlement...."

I told him I was laughing at him about that too.

"It was the correct thing to do, you know," were the words he shut the door upon. The ass....

The phrase of his—that he had thought of me at the moment of his fall—gives you at once the measure of his respect for me. But it gave me much more. It gave me my cue: it put it into my head to say he was debauched. And, indeed, that is debauchery. For it is the introduction of one's morals into the management of one's appetites that makes an indulgence of them debauchery. Had my friend Edward regarded his seduction as the thing he so much desired me to tell him it was; a thing of youth, high spirits—a thing we all do—had he so regarded it I could not really have called it debauchery. But—and this is the profound truth—the measure of debauchery is the amount of joy we get from the indulgence of our appetites. And the measure of joy we get is the amount of excitement: if it brings into play not only all our physical but all our moral nature, then we have the crucial point beyond which no man can go. It isn't, in fact, the professional seducer, the artist in seduction that gets pleasure from the pursuit of his avocation, any more than it is the professional musician who gets thrills from the performance of music. You cannot figure to yourself the violinist, as he fiddles the most complicated passage of a concerto, when he really surmounts the difficulty by dint of using all his knowledge and all his skill—you cannot imagine him thinking of his adviser, his mother, his God and all the other things that my young friend says he thought about. And it is the same with the professional seducer. He may do all that he knows to bring his object about—but that is not debauchery. It is, by comparison, a joyless occupation: it is drinking when you are thirsty. Putting it in terms of the most threadbare allegory—you cannot imagine that Adam got out of the fall the pleasure that Edward Burden got out of his bite of the apple.

But Edward Burden, whilst he shilly-shallied with "Shall I?" and "Shan't I?" could deliciously introduce into the matter *all* his human relationships. He could think of me, of his mother, of the fact that potentially he was casting to the winds the very cause for his existence. For assuredly, if Edward Burden have a cause for existence it is that he should not, morally or physically, do anything that would unfit him to make a good marriage. So he had, along with what physical pleasure there might be, the immense excitement of staking his all along with the tremendous elation of the debate within himself that went before. For he was actually staking his all upon the chance that he could both take what he desired and afterwards reconcile it with his conscience to make a good match. Well, he has staked and won. That is the true debauchery. That, in a sense, is the compensating joy that Puritanism gets.

V

I HAVE just come in. Again you will not guess from where. From choosing a motor car with Burden and his *fiancée*. It seems incredible that I should be called upon to preside at these preparations for my own execution. I looked at hundreds of these shiny engines, with the monstrously inflated white wheels, and gave a half-amused—but I can assure you a half-interested—attention to my own case. For one of these will one day—and soon now—be arrested in a long rush, by my extinction. In it there will be seated the two young people who went with me through the garages. They will sit in some sort of cushioned ease—the cushions will be green, or red, or blue in shiny leather. I think, however, that they will not be green—because Miss Averies let slip to me, in a little flutter of shy confidence, the words: "Oh, don't let's have green, because it's an unlucky colour." Edward Burden, of course, suppressed her with a hurried whisper as if, in thus giving herself away to me, she must be committing a sin against the house of Burden.

That, naturally, is the Burden tradition: a Burden's wife must possess frailties: but she must feign perfection even to a trusted adviser of the family. She must not confess to

41

superstitions. It was amusing, the small incident, because it was the very first attempt that little Miss Averies has ever made to get near me. God knows what Edward may have made me appear to her: but I fancy that, whatever Edward may have said, she had pierced through that particular veil: she realises, with her intuition, that I am dangerous. She is alarmed and possibly fascinated because she feels that I am not "straight"—that I might, in fact, be a woman or a poet. Burden, of course, has never got beyond seeing that I dress better than he does and choose a dinner better than his uncle Darlington.

I came, of course, out of the motor-car ordeal with flying colours—on these lines. I lived, in fact, up to my character for being orthodox in the matter of comfort. I even suggested two little mirrors, like those which were so comforting to us all when we sat in hansom cabs. That struck Burden as being the height of ingenuity—and I know it proved to Miss Averies, most finally, that I am dangerous, since no woman ever looks in those little mirrors without some small motive of coquetry. It was just after that that she said to me:

"Don't you think that the little measures on the tops of the new canisters are extravagant for China tea?"

That, of course, admitted me to the peculiar intimacy that women allow to other women, or to poets, or to dangerous men. Edward, I know, dislikes the drinking of China tea because it is against the principle of supporting the British flag. But Miss Averies in her unequal battle with this youth of the classical features slightly vulgarised, called me in to show a sign of sympathy—to give at least the flicker of the other side—of the woman, the poet, or the pessimist among men. She asked me, in fact, not to take up the cudgels to the extent of saying that China tea is the thing to drink—that would have been treason to Edward—but she desired that her instinct should be acknowledged to the extent of saying that the measures of canisters should be contrived to suit the one kind of tea as well as the other. In his blind sort of way Edward caught the challenge in the remark and his straight brows lowered a very little.

"If you don't have more than three pounds of China tea in the house in a year it won't matter about the measures," he said. "We never use more at Shackleton."

"But it makes the tea too strong, Edward."

"Then you need not fill the measure," he answered.

"Oh, I wish," she said to me, "that you'd tell Edward not to make me make tea at all. I dread it. The servants do it so much better."

"So," I asked, "Edward has arranged everything down to the last detail?"

Edward looked to me for approval and applause.

"You see, Annie has had so little experience, and I've had to look after my mother's house for years." His air said: "Yes! You'll see our establishment will be run on the very best lines! Don't you admire the way I'm taming her already?"

I gave him, of course, a significant glance. Heaven knows why: for it is absolutely true that I am tired of appearing reliable—to Edward Burden or anyone else in the world. What I want to do is simply to say to Edward Burden: "No, I don't at all admire your dragging down a little bundle of ideals and sentiments to your own fatted calf's level."

I suppose I have in me something of the poet. I can imagine that if I had to love or to marry this little Averies girl I should try to find out what was her tiny vanity and I should minister to it. In some way I should discover from her that she considered herself charming, or discreet, or tasteful, or frivolous, beyond all her fellows. And, having discovered it, I should bend all my energies to giving her opportunities for displaying her charm, her discreetness or her coquetry. With a woman of larger and finer mould—with you!—I should no doubt bring into play my own idealism. I should invest her with the attributes that I consider the most desirable in the world. But in either case I cannot figure myself dragging her down to my own social or material necessities.

That is what Edward Burden is doing for little Miss Averies. I don't mean to say that he does not idealise her—but he sees her transfigured as the dispenser of his special brand of tea or the mother of the sort of child that he was. And that seems to me a very valid reason why women, if they were wise, should trust their fortunes cold-bloodedly and of set reason to the class of dangerous men that now allure them and that they flee from.

They flee from them, I am convinced, because they fear for their worldly material fortunes. They fear, that is to say, that the poet is not a stable man of business: they recognise that he is a gambler—and it seems to them that it is folly to trust to a gambler for life-long protection. In that they are perhaps right. But I think that no woman doubts her power to retain a man's affection—so that it is not to the reputation for matrimonial instability that the poet owes his disfavour. A woman lives, in short, to play with this particular fire, since to herself she says: "Here is a man who has broken the hearts of many women. I will essay the adventure of taming him." And, if she considers the adventure a dangerous one, that renders the contest only the more alluring, since at heart every woman, like every poet, is a gambler. In that perhaps she is right.

But it seems to me that women make a great mistake in the value of the stakes they are ready to pay in order to enter this game. They will stake, that is to say, their relatively great coin—their sentimental lives; but they hoard with closed fingers the threepenny bit which is merely the material future.

They prefer, that is to say, to be rendered the mere presiding geniuses of well-loaded boards. It is better to be a lady—which you will remember philologically means a "loaf-cutter"—than to be an Ideal.

And in this they are obviously wrong. If a woman can

achieve the obvious miracle of making a dangerous man stable in his affections she may well be confident that she can persuade him to turn his serious attention to the task of keeping a roof over her head.

Certainly, I know, if I were a woman, which of the two types of men I would choose. Upon the lowest basis it is better for all purposes of human contracts to be married to a good liar than to a bad one. For a lie is a figurative truth—and it is the poet who is the master of these illusions. Even in the matter of marital relations it is probable that the poet is as faithful as the Edward Burdens of this world—only the Edward Burdens are more skilful at concealing from the rest of the world their pleasant vices. I doubt whether they are as skilful at concealing them from the woman concerned—from the woman, with her intuition, her power to seize fine shades of coolness and her awakened self-interest. Imagine the wife of Edward Burden saying to him, "You have deceived me!" Imagine then the excellent youth, crimsoning, stuttering. He has been taught all his life that truth must prevail though the skies fall—and he stammers: "Yes: I have betrayed you." And that is tragedy, though in the psychological sense—and that is the important one—Edward Burden may have been as faithful as the ravens, who live for fifteen decades with the same mate. He will, in short, blunder into a tragic, false position. And he will make the tragedy only the more tragic in that all the intellectual powers he may possess will be in the direction of perpetuating the dismal position. He will not be able to argue that he has not been unfaithful—but he will be able to find a hundred arguments for the miserable woman prolonging her life with him. Position, money, the interests of the children, the feelings of her family and of his—all these considerations will make him eloquent to urge her to prolong her misery. And probably she will prolong it.

This, of course, is due to the excellent Edward's lack of an instinctive sympathy. The poet, with a truer vision, will in the same case, be able to face his Miss Averies' saying, "You have deceived me!" with a different assurance. Supposing the deflection to have been of the momentary kind, he will be able to deny with a good conscience since he will be aware of himself and his feelings. He will at least be able to put the case in its just light. Or, if the deflection be really temperamental, really permanent, he will be unable— it being his business to look at the deeper verities—to lie himself out of the matter. He will break, strictly and sharply. Or, if he do not, it may be taken as a sign that his Miss Averies is still of value to him—that she, in fact, is still the woman that it is his desire to have for his companion. This is true of course, only in the large sense, since obviously there are poets whose reverence for position, the interest of children or the feelings of their friends and relatives, may outweigh their hatred of a false position. These, however, are poets in the sense that they write verse: I am speaking of those who live the poet's life; to such, a false position is too intolerable to be long maintained.

But this again is only one of innumerable side-issues: let me return to my main contention that a dinner of herbs with a dangerous man is better than having to consume the flesh of stalled oxen with Edward Burden. Perhaps that is only a way of saying that you would have done better to entrust yourself to me than to—(But no, your husband is a better man than Edward Burden. He has at least had the courage to revert to his passion. I went this afternoon to your chemists and formally notified them that if they supplied him with more than the exactly prescribed quantity of that stuff, I, as holding your power of attorney, should do all that the law allows me to do against them).

Even to the dullest of men, marrying is for the most part an imaginative act. I mean marrying as a step in life sanctioned by law, custom and that general consent of mankind which is the hall-mark of every irrational institution. By irrational I do not mean wrong or stupid. Marriage is august by the magnitude of the issues it involves, balancing peace and strife on the fine point of a natural impulse refined by the need of a tangible ideal. I am not speaking here of mere domestic peace or strife which for most people that count are a question of manners and a mode of life. And I am thinking of the peace mostly— the peace of the soul which yearns for some sort of certitude in this earth, the peace of the heart which yearns for conquest, the peace of the senses that dreads deception, the peace of the imaginative faculty which in its restless quest of a high place of rest is spurred on by these great desires and that great fear.

And even Edward Burden's imagination is moved by these very desires and that very fear—or else he would not have dreamt of marrying. I repeat, marriage is an imaginative institution. It's true that his imagination is a poor thing, but it is genuine nevertheless. The faculty of which I speak is of one kind in all of us. Not to every one is given that depth of feeling, that faculty of absolute trust which *will not* be deceived, and the exulting masterfulness of the senses which are the mark of a fearless lover. Fearless lovers are rare, if obstinate, and sensual fools are countless as grains of sand by the seashore. I can imagine that correct young man perfectly capable of setting himself deliberately to worry a distracted girl into surrender.

VI

I DON'T know why, to-night in particular, the fact that I am a dead man occurs to me very insistently. I had forgotten this for two whole days. If anyone very dear to you has ever been *in extremis* at a distance and you have journeyed to be at the last bedside, you will know how possible this is—how for hours at a time the mind will go wandering away from the main fact that is drawing you onwards, till suddenly it comes back: some one is dying at a distance. And I suppose one's I is the nearest friend that one has—and my I is dying at a distance. At the end of a certain number of days is the deathbed towards which I am hurrying—it is a fact which I cannot grasp. But one aspect grows more clear to me every time I return to this subject.

You remember that, when we have discussed suicide, we have agreed that to the man of action death is a solution: to the man of thought it is none. For the man of action expresses himself in action, and death is the negation of action: the man of thought sees the world only in thoughts, and over thought death exercises no solution of continuity. If one dies one's actions cease, one's problem continues. For that reason it is only in so far as I am a man of action that I shall be dying. You understand what I mean—for I do not mean that it is my actions that have killed me. It is simply because I have taken refuge from my thoughts in action, and because after April 5 that refuge will be closed to me, that I take refuge in a final action which, properly speaking, is neither action nor refuge.

And perhaps I am no man of action at all, since the action in which I have taken refuge is properly speaking no action at all, but merely the expression of a frame of mind. I have gambled, that is to say I have not speculated. For the speculator acts for gain: the gambler in order to interest himself. I have gambled—to escape from you: I have tried to escape from my thoughts of you into divining the undivinable future. For that is what gambling is. You try for a rise: you try for a fall—and the rise or the fall may depend on the momentary madness of a dozen men who declare a war, or upon the rain from heaven which causes so many more stalks of wheat to arise upon so many million square inches of earth. The point is that you make yourself dependent upon caprice—upon the caprice of the weather or upon the movement in the minds of men more insane than yourself.

To-day I have entered upon what is the biggest gamble of my whole life. Certain men who believe in me—they are not Edward Burdens, nevertheless they believe in me—have proposed to me to form a corner in a certain article which is indispensable to the daily life of the City. I do not tell you what it is because you will assuredly witness the effects of this inspiration.

You will say that, when this is accomplished, it will be utterly uninteresting. And that is literally true: when it is done it will be uninteresting. But in the multiplicity of things that will have to be done before the whole thing is done—in the waiting for things to take effect, in the failures perhaps more than in the successes, since the failures will imply new devising—in all the meticulous thought-readings that will be necessary, the interest will lie, and in the men with whom one is brought into contact, the men with whom one struggles, the men whom one must bribe or trick.

And you will say: How can I who am to die in fourteen days embark upon an enterprise that will last many months or many years? That, I think, is very simple.

It is my protest against being called a man of action, the misconception that I have had to resent all my life. And this is a thought: not an action: a thought made up of an almost infinite number of erring calculations. You have probably forgotten that I have founded two towns, upon the south coast: originated four railways in tropical climates and one in the West of England: and opened up heaven knows how many mines of one kind or another—and upon my soul I had forgotten these things too until I began to cast about in my mind. And now I go to my death unmindful of these glories in so far as they are concrete. In that sense my death is utter: it is a solution. But, in so far as they are my refuges from you they remain problems to which, if my ghost is to escape you, I must return again and again.

In dying I surrender to you and thus, for the inner self of myself, death is no ending but the commencement of who knows what tortures. It is only in the latent hope that death is the negation of consciousness that I shall take my life. For death, though it can very certainly end no problem, may at least make us unconscious of how, eventually, the problem solves itself. That, you see, is really the crux of the whole thing—that is why the man of action will take refuge in death: the man of thought, never. But I, I am the man of neither the one nor the other: I am the man of love, which partakes of action and of thought, but which is neither.

The lover is, perhaps, the eternal doubter—simply because there is no certain panacea for love. Travel may cure it—but travel may cause to arise homesickness, which of all forms of love is the most terrible. To mix with many other men may cure it—but again, to the man who really loves, it may be a cause for still more terrible unrest, since seeing other men and women may set one always comparing the beloved object with the same thing. And, indeed, the form that it takes with me—for with me love takes the form of a desire to discuss—the form which it takes with me renders each thing that I see, each man with whom I speak, the more torturing, since always I desire to adjust my thoughts of them by your thoughts.

I went down the other day—before I had begun to write these letters to you and before I knew death impended so nearly over me—to the sea at P—I was trying to get rid of you. I sat in the moonlight and saw the smacks come home, visible for a minute in the track of the moon and then no more than their lights in the darkness. The fishermen talked of death by drowning mostly: the passage of the boats across that trail of light suggested reflections, no doubt trite. But, without you to set my thoughts by, I could get no more forward: I went round and round in a ring from the corpses fished up in the nets to the track of the moon. And since walking up and down on the parade brought me no nearer to you, I did not even care to move: I neither meditated nor walked, neither thought nor acted. And that is real torture.

It was the next morning that I heard that young Burden desired that his *fiancée*'s solicitors should scrutinise the accounts of the Burden Trust—and Death loomed up before me.

You will ask: why Death? Why not some alternative? Flight or prison? Well: prison would be an unendurable travelling through Time, flight an equally unendurable travelling through Time with Space added. Both these things are familiar: Death alone, in spite of all the experience that humanity has had of Death, is the utterly unfamiliar. For a gambler it is a *coup* alluring beyond belief—as we know neither what we stake nor what we stand to win. I, personally, stand to win a great deal, since Life holds nothing for me and I stake only my life—and what I seek is only forgetfulness of you, or some sort of eventual and incomprehensible union with you. For the union with you that I seek is a queer sort of thing; hardly at all, I think, a union of the body, but a sort of consciousness of our thoughts proceeding onwards together. That we may find in the unending Afterwards. Or we may find the Herb Oblivion.

Either of these things I desire. For, in so far as we can dogmatise about Death we may lay it down that Death is the negation of Action but is powerless against Thought. I do not desire Action: and at the same time I do not fear Thought. For it is not my thoughts of you that I fear: left alone with them I can say: "What is she more than any other material object?" It is my feelings that wear out my brain—my feelings that make me know that you are more than every material object living or still, and more than every faith dead or surviving. For feeling is neither Thought nor Action: it is the very stuff of Life itself. And, if Death be the negation of Life it may well be the end of consciousness.

The worst that Death can do to me is to deliver me up for ever to unsatisfied longings for you. Well, that is all that Life has done, that is all that Life can do, for me.

But Life can do so much more that is worse. Believe me when I say that I dread imprisonment—and believe me when I say that I do not dread disgrace. For you know very well that it is true when I say that I positively chuckle at the thought of the shock my fall would give to all these unawakened intelligences of this world. You know how I despise Edward Burden for trusting in me; you know how I have always despised other people who trusted in established reputations. I don't mean to say that I should not have liked to keep the game up, certainly I should, since in gambling it is more desirable to win than to lose. And it is more amusing to fool fools than to give them eye-openers. But I think that, in gambling, it is only a shade less desirable, *per se*, to lose than to win. The main point is the sensation of either; and the only valid objection to losing is that, if one loses too often one has at last no longer the wherewithal to gamble. Similarly, to give people eye-openers is, *per se*, nearly as desirable as to fool them. It is not quite so desirable, since the game itself *is* the fooling. But the great objection in *my* case is that the eye-opener would once and for all put an end to the chance of my ever fooling them again. That, however, is a very small matter and what I dread is not that. If people no longer trusted in me I could no doubt still find an outlet for my energies with those who sought to take advantage of my abilities, trusting to themselves to wrest from me a sufficient share of the plunder that they so ardently desire, that I so really have no use for.

No, I seek in Death a refuge from exposure not because exposure would cripple my energies: it would probably help them: and not because exposure would mean disgrace; I should probably find ironical satisfaction in it—but simply because it would mean imprisonment. That I dread beyond belief: I clench my fingers when, in conversation; I hear the words: "A long sentence." For that would mean my being delivered up for a long time—for ever—to you. I write "for ever" advisedly and after reflection, since a long subjection without relief, to that strain would leave upon my brain a wound that must prove ineffaceable. For to be alone and to think—those are my terrors.

One reads that men who have been condemned for long years to solitary imprisonment go mad. But I think that even that sad gift from Omnipotent Fate would not be mine. As I figure the world to myself, Fate is terrible only to those who surrender to her. If I surrendered, to the extent of living to go to prison, then assuredly the future must be uniformly heavy, uniformly doomed, in my eyes. For I would as soon be mad as anything else I can think of. But I should not go mad. Men go mad because of the opportunities they miss: because the world changes outside their prison walls, or because their children starve. But I have no opportunities to miss or take: the changes of the world to me are nothing, and there is no soul between whom and starvation I could stand.

Whilst I am about making this final disposition of my properties—let me tell you finally what I have done in regard to your husband himself. It is a fact—and this I have been keeping up my sleeve as a final surprise for you—that he is almost cured....

But I have just received an incomprehensible note from Edward Burden. He asks me for some particulars as to his confounded estate and whether I can lend him some thousands of pounds at short notice. Heaven knows what new scrape this is that he's in. Of course this may precipitate *my crash*. But whatever happens, I shall find time to write my final words to you—and nothing else really matters....

VII

I HAVEN'T yet discovered what Edward Burden is doing. I have found him a good round sum upon mortgage—the irony of the position being that the money is actually his whilst the mortgage does not actually exist. He says that what he is doing with the money will please me. I suppose that means that he's embarking upon some sort of speculation which he imagines that I would favour. It is odd that he should think that I find gratification in his imitating myself.

But why should I concern myself with this thing at all? Nothing in the world can ever please or displease me any more. For I have taken my resolve: this is my last night upon earth. When I lay down this pen again, I shall never take up any pen more. For I have said all that I can say to you. I am utterly tired out. To-night I shall make up into a parcel all these letters—I must sit through the night because it is only to-morrow morning that I shall be able to register the parcel to you—and registering it will be my last act upon the habitable globe. For biting through the glass in the ring will be not an action, but the commencement of a new train of thought. Or perhaps only my final action will come to an end when you read these words in

Rome. Or will that be only thought—the part of me that lives—pleading to you to give your thoughts for company? I feel too tired to think the matter out!

Let me, then, finish with this earth: I told you, when I finished writing last night, that Robert is almost cured. I would not have told you this for the sake of arrogating to myself the position of a saviour. But I imagine that you would like the cure to go on and, in the case of some accident after my death, it might go all to pieces once more. Quite simply then: I have been doing two things. In the first place I have persuaded your chemists to reduce very gradually the strength of chloral, so that the bottles contain nearly half water. And Robert perceives no difference. Now of course it is very important that he shall not know of the trick that is being so beneficently played on him—so that, in case he should go away or for one reason or another change his chemists, it must be carefully seen to that instead of pure chloral he obtains the exactly diluted mixture. In this way he may be brought gradually to drinking almost pure water.

But that alone would hardly be satisfactory: a comparatively involuntary cure is of little value in comparison with an effort of the will. You may, conceivably, expel nature with a fork, but nothing but a passion will expel a passion. The only point to be proved is whether there exists in your husband any other passion for the sake of which he might abandon his passion for the clearness of vision which he always says his chloral gives him. He has not, of course, the incentives usual to men: you cannot, in fact, "get" him along ordinary lines....But apart from his physical craving for the drug he *has* that passion for clearness of intellect that he says the drug gives him—and it is through that that, at last, I have managed to hit his pride.

For I have put it to him very strongly that one view of life is just as good as another—no better, no worse, but just the same. And I have put it to him that his use of chloral simply limits for him the number of views of life that he might conceivably have. And, when you come to think of all the rhapsodies of his that we have listened to, I think that that piece of special pleading is sufficiently justified. I do indeed honestly believe that, for what it is worth, he is on the road to salvation. He means to make a struggle—to attempt the great feat of once more seeing life with the eyes that Fate originally gave to him.

This is my legacy to *you*: if you ask me why I have presented you with this man's new identity—since it *will* mean a new identity—I must answer that I simply don't know. Why have we kept him alive all these years? I have done it no doubt because I had nothing to give you. But you? If you have loved me you must have wished him—I won't say dead—but no more there. Yet you have tried too—and I suppose this answer to the riddle is simply the answer to the whole riddle of our life. We have tried to play a supremely difficult game simply because it sanctified our love. For, after all, sanctification arises from difficulties. Well, we have made our way very strait and we have so narrowed the door of entrance that it has vanished altogether. We have never had *any* hope of a solution that could have satisfied us. If we had cared to break the rules of the game, I suppose we could have done it easily enough—and we could have done it the more easily since neither you nor I ever subscribed to those rules. If we have not it was, I think, simply because we sought the difficulty which sanctifies.... Has it been a very imbecile proceeding? I am most uncertain. For it is not a thing to be very proud of—to be able to say that, for a whole lifetime, one has abstained from that which one most desired. On the other hand, we have won a curious and difficult game. Well—there it is—and there is your legacy. I do not think that there is anything else for me to write about. You will see that, in my will, I have left everything I possess to—Edward Burden. This is not because I wish to make him reparation, and it's not because I wish to avoid scandal: it is simply because it may show him—one very simple thing. It will show him how very nearly I might have made things come right. I have been balancing my accounts very carefully, and I find that, reckoning things reasonably against myself, Edward Burden will have a five-pound note with which to buy himself a mourning-ring.

The being forced to attend to my accounts will make him gasp a good deal. It will certainly shake his belief in all accepted reputations—for he will look on the faces of many men each "as solid as the Bank of England," and he will think: "I wonder if you are like ——?" His whole world will crumble—not because I have been dishonest, since he is cold-blooded enough to believe that all men may be dishonest. But he will tremble because I have been able to be so wildly dishonest and yet to be so successfully respectable. He won't even dare to "expose" me, since, if he did that, half of the shares which he will inherit from me would suffer an eclipse of disreputability, would tumble to nothingness in value—and would damage his poor pocket. He will have to have my estate set down at a high figure; he will have to be congratulated on his fortunate inheritance, and he will have, sedulously, to compound my felony.

You will wonder how I can be capable of this final cruelty—the most cruel thing that, perhaps, ever one man did to another. I will tell you why it is: it is because I hate all the Edward Burdens of the world—because, being the eternal Haves of the world, they have made their idiotic rules of the game. And you and I suffer: you and I, the eternal Have Nots. And we suffer, not because their rules bind us, but because, being the finer spirits, we are forced to set ourselves rules that are still more strict in order that, in all things, we may be the truly gallant.

But why do I write: "You will wonder how I can be capable of this"? You will have understood—you who understand everything.

Eight in the morning.—Well: now we part. I am going to register the parcel containing all these letters to you. We part: and it is as if you were dropping back—the lost Eurydice of the world—into an utter blackness. For, in a minute, you will be no more than part of my past. Well then: goodnight.

VIII

YOU will have got the telegram I sent you long before you got the parcel of letters: you will have got the note I wrote you by the same post as the letters themselves. If I have taken these three days to myself before again writing to you it has been because I have needed to recover my power of thinking. Now, in a way, I have recovered it— and it is only fair to say that I have devoted all my thoughts to how the new situation affects you—and you in your relations to me.

It places me in your hands—let that be written first and foremost. You have to decree my life or my death. For I take it that now we can never get back again into our old position: I have spoken, you have heard me speak. The singular unity, the silence of our old life is done with for good. There is perhaps no reason why this should not be so: silence is no necessary part of our relationship. But it has seemed to make a rather exquisite bond between us.

It must, if I am to continue to live—it must be replaced by some other bond. In our silence we have seemed to speak in all sorts of strange ways: we have per- haps read each other's thoughts. I have seen words form themselves upon your lips. But now you must—there is no way out of it—you *must* write to me. You must write to me fully: all your thoughts. You must, as I have done, find the means of speech—or I can no longer live....

I am reprieved!

I don't know if, in my note to you, I explained exactly what had happened. It was in this way. I was anxious to be done with my world very early and, as soon as eight o'clock struck, I set out for the post-office at the corner to register that parcel of letters for you. Till the task was accomplished—the last I was to perform on earth—I noticed nothing: I was simply in a hurry. But, having given the little faggot into the hands of a sleepy girl, I said to myself suddenly: "Now I *am* dead!" I began suddenly as they say of young children, to "notice." A weight that I had never felt before seemed to fall away from me. I noticed, precisely, that the girl clerk was sleepy, that, as she reached up one hand to take the parcel over the brass caging, she placed the other over her mouth to hide a yawn.

And out on the pavement it was most curious what had befallen the world. It had lost all interest: but it had become fascinating, vivid. I had not, you see, any senses left, but my eyesight and hearing. Vivid: that is the word. I watched a news-boy throw his papers down an area, and it appeared wonderfully interesting to discover that *that* was how one's papers got into the house. I watched a milkman go up some doorsteps to put a can of milk beside a boot-scraper and I was wonderfully interested to see a black cat follow him. They were the clearest moments I have ever spent upon the earth—those when I was dead. They were so clear because nothing else weighed on my attention but just those little things. It was an extraordinary, a luxuriant feeling. That, I imagine, must have been how Adam and Eve felt before they had eaten of the fruit of knowledge.

Supposing I had tacitly arranged with myself that I would die in the street, I think I should still have walked home simply to dally longer with that delightful feeling of sheer curiosity. For it was sheer curiosity to see how this world, which I had never looked at, really performed before utterly unbiassed eyes.

That was why, when I got home, I sent away the messenger that brought to me Edward Burden's letter; there was to be no answer. Whatever Burden's query might be I was not going to commit myself to any other act. My last was that of sending off the parcel to you.

My opening Burden's letter when the messenger had gone was simply a part of my general curiosity. I wanted to see how a Burden letter would look when it no longer had any bearings at all for me. It was as if I were going to read a letter from that dear Edward to a man I did not know upon a subject of which I had never heard.

And then I was reprieved!

The good Edward, imagining that I was hurt at his having proposed to allow his wife's solicitors to superintend my stewardship—the good Edward in his concern had positively insisted that all the deeds should be returned to me absolutely unchecked. He said that he had had a hard fight for it and that the few thousands he had borrowed from me had represented his settlement, which he had thus paid in specie....

It chimed in wonderfully with his character, when I come to think of it. Of course he was disciplining Miss Averies' representatives just as he had disciplined her in the matter of China tea of which I have written to you. And he had imagined that I was seriously hurt! Can you figure to yourself such an imbecile?

But, if you permit me to continue to live, you will be saving the poor fool from the great shock I had prepared for him—the avalanche of discovery, the earthquake of uncertainty. For he says in that so kind way of his that, having thus shown his entire confidence in me—in the fact, that is, that Providence is on the side of all Burdens—he will choose a time in the future, convenient for me, when he will go thoroughly with me into his accounts. And inasmuch as his wedding-tour will take him all round the world I have at least a year in which to set things straight. And of course I can put off his scrutiny indefinitely or deceive him for ever.

I did not think all these things at once. In fact, when I had read his letter, so strong within me was the feeling that it was only a mental phenomenon, a thing that had no relation with me—the feeling of finality was so strong upon me that I actually found myself sitting in that chair before I realised what had occurred.

What had occurred was that I had become utterly and for good your property.

In that sense only am I reprieved. As far as Edward Burden is concerned I am entirely saved. I stand before you and ask you to turn your thumb up or down. For, having spoken as I have to you, I have given you a right over me. Now that the pressing necessity for my death is over I have to ask you whether I shall plunge into new adventures that will lead me to death or whether I am to find some medium in which we may lead a life of our own, in some way together. I was about to take my life to avoid prison: now prison is no more a part of my scheme of existence. But I must now have some means of working towards you or I must run some new and wild risk to push you out of my thoughts. I don't, as you know, ask you to be my secret mistress, I don't ask you to elope with me. But I say that you *must* belong to me as much in thought as I have, in this parcel of letters, been revealed and given over to you. Otherwise, I must once more gamble—and having tasted of gambling in the shadow of death, I must gamble for ever in that way. I must, I mean, feel that I am coming towards you or committing crimes that I may forget you.

My dear, I am a very tired man. If you knew what it was to long for you as I have longed for you all these years, you would wonder that I did not, sitting in that chair, put the ring up to my teeth, in spite of Burden's letter, and end it. I have an irresistible longing for rest—or perhaps it is only your support. To think that I must face for ever—or for as long as it lasts—this troublesome excitement of avoiding thoughts of you—that was almost unbearable. I resisted because I had written these letters to you. I love you and I know you love me—yet without them I would have inflicted upon you the wound of my death. Having written them I cannot face the cruelty to you. I mean that, if I had died without your knowing why, it would have been only a death grievous to you—still it is the duty of humanity and of you with humanity to bear and to forget deaths. But now that you must know, I could not face the cruelty of filling you with the pain of unmerited remorse. For I know that you would have felt remorse, and it would have been unmerited, since I gave you no chance or any time to stretch out your hands to me. Now I give it you and wait for your verdict.

For the definite alternatives are these: I will put Burden's estate absolutely clear within the year and work out, in order to make safe money, the new and comparatively sober scheme of which I have written to you: that I will do if you will consent to be mine to the extent of sharing our thoughts alone. Or, if you will not, I will continue to gamble more wildly than ever with the Burden money. And that in the end means death and a refuge from you.

So then, I stand reprieved—and the final verdict is in your hands.

APPENDIX
A NOTE ON ROMANCE

WRITING to his collaborator in a letter published in the *Transatlantic Review* for January 1924, Mr. Conrad makes the following ascriptions of passages in the work above-named:

"First Part, yours; Second Part, mainly yours, with a little by me on points of seamanship and suchlike small matters; Third Part, about 60 per cent. mine with important touches by you; Fourth Part, mine, with here and there an important sentence by you; Fifth Part practically all yours, including the famous sentence at which we both exclaimed: 'This is Genius,' (Do you remember what it is?) with perhaps half a dozen lines by me...."

Mr. Conrad's recollections—except for the generosity of his two "importants"—tally well enough with those of his collaborator if conception alone is concerned. When it comes, however, to the writing, the truth is that Parts One, Two, Three and Five are a singular mosaic of passages written alternately by one or other of the collaborators. The matchless Fourth Part is both in conception and writing entirely the work of Mr. Conrad.

Below will be found the analysis of *Romance*. Any student of literature with an ear for prose will hardly need these underlinings, for Mr. Conrad's definitenesses of statement stand out amongst his collaborator's more English keyings down, so that when one of his half-sentences bursts into the no doubt suaver prose of the other it is as if the page comes to life and speaks.

Every collaboration is a contest of temperaments if it be at all thoroughly carried out; and this collaboration was carried out so thoroughly that, even when the book came to the proof stage, the original publishers, half-way through the printing, sent the MS. back to the authors. They were still making innumerable corrections.

Originally conceived, in the attempt to convey realistically a real story of adventure recorded in a State Trial, as the thin tale of a very old man—and this before the question of collaboration arose—the book contains of its first version only the two opening sentences—and the single other sentence: "And, looking back, we see Romance!" In between lay, to say the least of it, almost unbelievable labours—a contest of attrition lasting over several years. For in so far as this collaboration was a contest of wills it was a very friendly one; yet it was the continual attempt on the part of the one collaborator to key up and of the other to key down. And so exhausting was the contest that in the course of the years two definite breakdowns occurred. In the first the robuster writer let the book called *The Inheritors* just go and it remains a monument as it were of silverpoint, delicacies and allusiveness. The second breakdown is recorded in the Fourth Part of *Romance*, sketches for which were written over and over—and then over—again, until the weaker brother, in absolute exhaustion, in turn let it go at that. So, to mark those breaking points, you have the silver-point of *The Inheritors* set against the, let us say, oil-painting of this matchless Fourth Part.

The Nature of a Crime should have become a novel treating of the eternal subject of the undetected criminal—a theme which every writer for once or twice in his life at least contemplates in a world in which the fortunate are so very often the merely not found out. The courage of few writers carries them even beyond the contemplation; in this case the joint courages of the authors went as far as what you may read.

The passage from the Fifth Part of *Romance* printed below contains the "famous sentence" as to which Mr. Conrad writes: "We both exclaimed: 'This is genius.'"

(Joseph Conrad in Roman type; F. M. Ford in Italics.)
Part One: Chapter One.
To yesterday and to-day I say my polite "vaya usted con dios." What are these days to me? But that far-off day of my romance, when from between *the blue and the white bales in Don Ramon's darkened storeroom, at Kingston*, I saw the door open before the figure of *an old man with the tired, long, white face*, that day I am not likely to forget. I remember *the chilly smell of the typical West Indian store*, the indescribable

smell of lamp gloom, of locos, of pimento, of olive oil, of new sugar, of new rum; the glassy double sheen of Ramon's great spectacles, the piercing eyes in the mahogany face, while the tap, tap, tap of a cane on the flags went on behind the inner door; *the click of the latch; the stream of light.* The door, petulantly thrust inwards, struck against some barrels. I remember the rattling of the bolts on that door, and *the tall figure* that appeared there, *snuff-box in hand. In that land of white clothes that precise, ancient Castilian in black was something to remember. The black cane that had made the tap, tap, tap dangled by a silken cord from the hand whose delicate blue-veined wrinkled wrist ran back into a foam of lawn ruffles.* The other hand paused in the act of conveying a pinch of snuff to the nostrils of the *hooked nose that had, on the skin stretched tight over the bridge, the polish of old ivory; the elbow pressing the black cocked hat against the side; the legs, one bent, the other bowing a little back*—this was the attitude of Seraphina's father.

Having imperiously thrust the door of the inner room open, he remained immovable, with no intention of entering, and called in a harsh, aged voice: "Señor Ramon! Señor Ramon!" And then twice: "Seraphina! Seraphina!" turning his head back.

Then for the first time I saw Seraphina, looking over her father's shoulder. I remember her face of that day; *her eyes were grey—the grey of black, not of blue. For a moment they looked me straight in the face, reflectively, unconcerned, and then travelled to the spectacles of old Ramon.*

This glance—remember I was young on that day—had

been enough to set me wondering what they were thinking of me; what they could have seen of me.

"But there he is—your Señor Ramon," she said to her father, *as if she were chiding him for a petulance in calling;* "your sight is not very good, my poor little father—there he is, your Ramon."

The warm reflection of the light behind her, gilding the curve of her face from ear to chin, lost itself in the shadows of black lace falling from dark hair that was not quite black. She spoke as if the words clung to her lips; as if she had to put them forth delicately for fear of damaging the frail things.

Part One: Chapter Five.

Macdonald cleared his throat, with a sound resembling the coughing of a defective pump, and a mere trickle of a voice asked:

"Hwhat evidence have ye of identitee?"

I hadn't any at all and began to finger my buttonholes as shamefaced as a pauper before a Board. The certitude dawned upon me suddenly that Carlos, even if he would consent to swear to me, would prejudice my chances.

I cannot help thinking that *I came very near to being cast adrift upon the streets of Kingston. To my asseverations Macdonald returned nothing but a series of minute "humphs." I don't know what overcame his scruples; he had shown no signs of yielding, but suddenly turning on his heel* made a motion with one of his flabby white hands. I understood it to mean that I was to follow him aft.

The decks were covered with a jabbering turmoil of

negroes with muscular arms and brawny shoulders. All their shining faces seemed to be momentarily gashed open to show rows of white, and were spotted with inlaid eye-balls. The sounds coming from them were a bewildering noise. They were hauling baggage about aimlessly. *A large soft bundle of bedding nearly took me off my legs.* There wasn't room for emotion. Macdonald laid about him with the handle of the umbrella a few inches from the deck; but the passage that he made for himself closed behind him.

Suddenly in the pushing and hurrying I came upon a little clear space beside a pile of boxes. Stooping over them was the angular fig-ure of Nichols, the second mate. He looked up at me, screwing his yellow eyes together.

"Going ashore," he asked, *"'long of that Puffing Billy?"*

"What business is it of yours?" I mumbled sulkily.

Sudden and intense threatening came into his yellow eyes.

"Don't you ever come to you know where," *he said; I don't want no spies on what I do. There's a man there'll crack your little backbone if he catches you. Don't yeh come now. Never."*

Part Four: Chapter One.

In my anxiety to keep clear of the schooner which, for all I know to this day, may not have been there at all, I had come too close to the sand, so close that I heard soft, rapid footfalls stop short in the fog. A voice seemed to be asking me in a whisper:

"Where, oh, where?"

Another cried out irresistibly, "I see it."

It was a subdued cry, as if hushed in sudden awe.

My arm swung to and fro; the turn of my wrist went on imparting the propelling motion of the oar. All the rest of my body was gripped helplessly in the dead expectation of the end, as if in the benumbing seconds of a fall from a towering height. And it was swift, too. I felt a draught at the back of my neck—a breath of wind. And instantly, as if a battering-ram had been let swing past me at many layers of stretched gauze, I beheld, through a tattered deep hole in the fog, a roaring vision of flames, borne down and springing up again; a dance of purple gleams on the strip of unveiled water, and three coal-black figures in the light.

One of them stood high on lank black legs, with long black arms thrown up stiffly above the black shape of a hat. The two others crouched low on the very edge of the water, peering as if from an ambush.

The clearness of this vision was contained by a thick and fiery atmosphere, into which a soft white rush and swirl of fog fell like a sudden whirl of snow. It closed down and overwhelmed at once the tall flutter of the flames, the black figures, the purple gleams playing round my oar. The hot glare had struck my eyeballs once, and that melted away again into the old, fiery stain on the mended fabric of the fog. But the attitudes of the crouching men left no room for doubt that we had been seen. I expected a sudden uplifting of voices on the shore, answered by cries from the sea, and I screamed excitedly at Castro to lay hold of his oar.

He did not stir, and after my shout, which must have fallen on the scared ears with a weird and unearthly note, a profound silence attended us—the silence of a superstitious fear. And, instead of howls, I heard, before the boat had travelled its own short length, a voice that seemed to be the voice of fear itself asking, "Did you hear that?" and a trembling mutter of an invocation to all the saints. Then a strangled throat trying to pronounce firmly, "The souls of the dead Inglez. Crying from pain."

Admiral Rowley's seamen, so miserably thrown away in the ill-conceived attack on the bay, were making a ghostly escort for our escape. Those dead boats'-crews were supposed to haunt the fatal spot, after the manner of spectres that linger in remorse, regret, or revenge, about the gates of departure. I had blundered; the fog, breaking apart, had betrayed us. But my obscure and vanquished countrymen held possession of the outlet by the memory of their courage. In this critical moment it was they, I may say, who stood by us.

We, on our part, must have been disclosed, dark, indistinct, utterly inexplicable; completely unexpected; an apparition of stealthy shades. The painful voice in the fog said again:

"Let them be. Answer not. They shall pass on, for none of them died on the shore—all in the water. Yes, all in the water."

Part Five: Chapter One.

"Why have I been brought here, your worships?" I asked with a great deal of firmness.

There were two figures in black, the one beside, the other behind a large black table. I was placed in front of them between two soldiers, in the centre of a large, gaunt room, with bare, dirty walls, and the arms of Spain above the judge's seat.

"You are before the Juez de la Primiera Instancia," said the *man in black beside the table. He wore a large and shadowy tricorn.* *"Be silent, and respect the procedure."*

It was, without doubt, excellent advice. *He whispered some words in the ear of the judge of the First Instance. It was plain enough to me that the judge was quite an inferior official, who merely decided whether there was any case against the accused;* he had, even to his clerk, an air of timidity, of doubt.

I said: "But I insist on knowing...."

The clerk said: "In good time...." *And then,* in the same tone of disinterested official routine, *he spoke to the Lugareño, who, from beside the door,* rolled very frightened eyes *from the judges and the clerk to myself and the soldiers*—"Advance."

The judge, in a hurried, perfunctory voice, put questions to the Lugareño; the clerk scratched with a large quill on a sheet of paper.

"Where do you come from?"

"The town of Rio Medio, excellency."

"Of what occupation?"

"Excellency—a few goats...."

"Why arc you here?"

"My daughter, excellency, married Pepe of the posada in the Calle...."

The judge said, "Yes, yes," with an unsanguine impatience. The Lugareño's dirty hands jumped nervously on the large rim of his limp hat.

"You lodge a complaint against the señor there."

The clerk pointed the end of his quill towards me.

"I? God forbid, excellency," the Lugareño *bleated.* "The Alguazil of the Criminal Court instructed me to be watchful.... "

Part Five: The End.

A long time after, a harsh voice said:

"Your excellency, we retire, of course, from the prosecution."

A different one directed:

"Gentlemen of the jury, you will return a verdict of 'Not Guilty'...."

Down below they were cheering uproariously because my life was saved. But it was I that had to face my saved life. I sat there, my head bowed into my hands. The old judge was speaking to me in a tone of lofty compassion:

"You have suffered much, as it seems, but suffering is the lot of us men. Rejoice now that your character is cleared; that here in this public place you have received the verdict of your countrymen that restores you to the liberties of our country and the affection of your kindred. I rejoice with you who am a very old man at the end of my life...."

It was rather tremendous, his deep voice, his weighted words. Suffering is the lot of us men.... The formidable legal array, the great powers of a nation, had stood up to teach me that, and they had taught me that—suffering is the lot of us men!

• • • • • • •

It takes long enough to realise that someone is dead at a dis-
tance. I had done that. But, how long, how long it needs to know
that the life of your heart has come back from the dead. For years
afterwards I could not bear to have her out of my sight.

Of our first meeting in London all I can remember is a
speechlessness that was like the awed hesitation of our
overtried souls before the greatness of a change from the
verge of despair to the opening of a supreme joy. The
whole world, the whole of life, with her return had
changed all round me; it enveloped me, it enfolded me so
lightly as not to be felt, so suddenly as not to be believed
in, so completely that that whole meeting was an
embrace, so softly that at last it lapsed into a sense of rest
that was like the fall of a beneficent and welcome death.

For suffering is the lot of man, but not inevitable failure or
worthless despair which is without end—suffering, the
mark of manhood, which bears within its pain a hope of
felicity like a jewel set in iron....

Her first words were:

"You broke our compact. You went away from me
whilst I was sleeping." Only the deepness of her reproach
revealed the depth of her love, and the suffering she too
had endured to reach a union that was to be without
end—and to forgive.

And, looking back, we see Romance—that subtle thing that is
mirage—that is life. It is the goodness of the years we have lived through,
of the old time when we did this or that, when we dwelt here or there.

APPENDIX

Looking back it seems a wonderful enough thing that I who am this and she who is that, commencing so far away a life that, after such sufferings borne together and apart, ended so tranquilly there in a world so stable—that she and I should have passed through so much, good chance and evil chance, sad hours and joyful, all lived down and swept away into the little heap of dust that is a life. That, too, is Romance.

THE NATURE OF A CRIME
NOTES

The English Review (p.7): During 1908-9, Ford established and edited the *English Review*, the first English modernist magazine. The first issue was prepared for the press at Conrad's home, Someries. Both Conrad and his wife wrote accounts of Ford and his editorial team arriving unexpectedly and working through the night to put the first issue together. See Jessie Conrad, *Joseph Conrad and His Circle* (London: Jarrolds, 1935), p.131; Joseph Conrad, letter to Ford Madox Ford (23 October 1923), most of which Ford published in the first issue of the *transatlantic review* (January 1924), pp.98-9 (See *The Collected Letters of Joseph Conrad* (Cambridge: Cambridge University Press, 2008), vol. 8, pp.205-6; and Jocelyn Baines, *Joseph Conrad: A Critical Biography* (Harmondsworth: Penguin Books, 1971), pp.418-9.

jouisseurs (p.7): sensualists.

little blue flower (p.8):The "blue flower" symbolised the object of yearning for German Romanticists. Novalis's fragmentary novel *Heinrich von Ofterdingen* (1802), which narrates the quest of its eponymous medieval hero, introduced the symbol of the search for the blue flower of happiness. Joseph von Eichendorff published a short poem "*Die blaue Blume*" ("The blue flower") (1818), which summarises this quest: "*Ich suche die blaue Blume,/Ich suche und finde sie nie/ ...*" (I search for the blue flower/ I search and do not find it/ ...). For Novalis, the blue flower represented a condition of happiness resulting from an overwhelming synaesthetic experience involving all the senses in a feeling of mystical (rather than erotic) love.

in articulo mortis (p.8): (Latin) at the moment of death. A confession made at the point of death is particularly significant in Catholicism, since it is necessary to die in a state of grace in order to avoid damnation.

I forgot, literally, all the books I had ever written (p.9): In June 1916, while serving with the Welch Regiment at Bécourt Wood, Ford was blown into the air by a high-explosive shell and suffered concussion. As a result, he suffered a complete loss of memory—for a while not even knowing his own name. This experience is repeated by Christopher Tietjens, in *Parade's End*: after similarly suffering shellshock, he has to re-stock his memory by reading the *Encyclopaedia Britannica*, whose inaccuracies he had previously corrected from memory. See also Ford's *Mightier Than the Sword* for a later account of this experience (London George Allen & Unwin, 1938), pp.265-6.

of Kent, of Sussex, of Carcassone—of New York, even (p.9)
Ford spent a decade in Kent from 1894, after his marriage
to Elsie Martindale; he lived in Sussex with Violet Hunt in
1914, writing part of *The Good Soldier* at Selsey, and with
Stella Bowen during 1920-21, writing *That Same Poor Man*
and parts of *No Enemy* at Pulborough; he visited Carcassone with Violet Hunt in 1912, while writing *The Young
Lovell*; he visited New York, Boston and Philadelphia with
Elsie in 1906, and wrote *Privy Seal* during this trip.

Romance (p.9): Published in 1903, *Romance* was a genuine
collaboration between Conrad and Ford. Ford had been
working on a novel "Seraphina". Within a month of their
first meeting in September 1898, Conrad and Ford had
agreed to collaborate on a re-working of the material.

in a certain periodical (p.9): *transatlantic review* (January, 1924).
This was the first issue of Ford's second magazine. The
poetry section included work by Ezra Pound and e.e.
cummings; the prose section included a story by Robert
McAlmon, a "letter" from Philippe Soupault and the first
half of "The Nature of a Crime". See Bernard J. Poli,
Ford Madox Ford and the Transatlantic Review (Syracuse, NY:
Syracuse University Press, 1967). This analysis appeared
as "A Note on *Romance*" as an appendix at the end of the
first book edition of the novel (Duckworth, 1924) and is
included in the present volume.

the Belgian coast (p.10): In July 1890, Ford, his wife and his two daughters went to Bruges. Conrad followed later in the month with his wife and son, once *Lord Jim* was completed, and the two families moved on to Knocke-sur-Mer. The idea was that Ford and Conrad would work together on "Seraphina", but Borys Conrad's dysentery and Conrad's gout put paid to any writing. The two families returned to England in late August.

Guido Fawkes (p.11): this was the name adopted by Guy Fawkes (1570-1606) when he fought for Catholic Spain against the Protestant Dutch. Guy Fawkes subsequently joined the group of English Catholics, led by Robert Catesby, who planned to assassinate James I and put a Catholic on the English throne. Fawkes was in charge of the gunpowder placed in an undercroft beneath the House of Lords. After a tip off, he was discovered and arrested on 5 November 1605—and charged with high treason.

peine forte et dure (p.11): (Fr. "strong and hard punishment"). Under English law, those accused of felony who remained silent were liable to *peine forte et dure*. This punishment ranged from imprisonment to being pressed under stones. It did not apply to treason cases: in treason cases, silence was interpreted as guilt. At trial, Guy Fawkes pleaded "not guilty".

another reign (p.12): ie Victoria.

seven pillars of the Forum (p.13): The Roman Forum is situated in the valley between the Palatine and Capitoline hills. Originally a marsh, the area was drained by the construction of the Cloaca Maxima (Great Drain) to create a marketplace. With the addition of temples, law courts and the Senate House, it became the centre of Rome's commercial and public life. Ford's narrator is referring to one of these temples, the Temple of Saturn, founded in 497 BCE and reconstructed in 42 BCE. It actually has eight pillars, although in photographs and drawings it often looks as if there are only seven.

the bronze she-wolf (p.13): Romulus and Remus, the legendary founders of Rome, were the twin sons of the Vestal priestess Rhea Silvia and Mars, the god of war. Left to die, they were suckled by a she-wolf. The bronze statue, the Capitoline Wolf, is the iconic representation of the city and its founding legend. Long thought to be of Etruscan origin, it is now thought to be a thirteenth-century bronze she-wolf with the figures of the twins added in the fifteenth century.

Gordon Square (p.15): in Bloomsbury. Developed by Thomas Cubitt in the 1820s, it later became associated with the Bloomsbury Group after Vanessa Bell moved there in 1904. Lytton Strachey lived at 51 Gordon Square.

K.C. (p.15): i.e. King's Counsel. After the 1830s, this was a status conferred by the Crown on barristers to recognise them as senior members of the profession. Initially, a King's Counsel or Queen's Counsel (depending on the gender of the ruling monarch), who was appointed to conduct court work on behalf of the Crown, was confined to the prosecution.

Natural History Museum (p.15): in Cromwell Road, South Kensington. This was established from the holdings of the natural history departments of the British Museum. Work on the building began in 1873, and the building was completed in 1880. The move of material from the British Museum began the following year and was completed by 1883.

Seaford Railway Bill (p.15): The Eastbourne, Seaford and Newhaven Railway Bill was introduced during the 1886 session of Parliament but was not successful.

You are of all time (p.18): c.f. Walter Pater's famous description of the Mona Lisa in his essay on Leonardo da Vinci in *The Renaissance* (1873): "All the thoughts and experience of the world have etched and moulded there ... She is older than the rocks among which she sits". In Conrad's late novel *The Arrow of Gold* (1919), the painter Henri Allègre responds in the same way to Rita: "I saw in that woman something of the women of all time" (*The Arrow of Gold* [London: Dent, 1924], p.28)

Zola (p.24): Emile Zola (1840-1902), French Naturalist novelist. Zola was also politically active and was particularly prominent during the Dreyfus case, when Alfred Dreyfus was falsely accused of selling military secrets to the Germans and convicted of treason. In *Return to Yesterday* (London: Victor Gollancz, 1931), Ford recalls meeting a very depressed Zola in London "at the time of his exile during the Dreyfus case" (283). He also recounts how he was once "riding with him in a hansom cab", when he noticed that Zola was "counting the numbers on the registration plates of the cabs that were in front of us": "If the added digits came to nine—or possibly to seven—he was momentarily elated; if they came to some inauspicious number—to thirteen I suppose—he would be prolongedly depressed" (284).

Johnson (p.24): Dr Samuel Johnson (1709-84), poet, essayist, biographer, lexicographer. Johnson suffered from depression and manifested an array of tics and mannerisms, including obsessive-compulsive rituals such as post-touching, associated with Tourette's syndrome. Ford read Johnson's work and Boswell's *Life of Dr Johnson*, which documents his various mannerisms, when he was recovering from his breakdown in 1905. See Max Saunders, *Ford Madox Ford: A Dual Life* (Oxford: Oxford University Press, 1996), 194.

an outlaw (p.26): Not identified.

Tristan and Isolde (p.32): The opera *Tristan und Isolde*, by

Richard Wagner (1813-87), was written between 1854 and 1859, but had to wait until June 1865 for its premiere in Munich. Its first production outside Germany was at the Theatre Royal, Drury Lane, in 1882, and its first Covent Garden production was in 1884. Tristan is entrusted with accompanying Isolde on her journey from Ireland to marry his uncle, King Mark, in Cornwall. At the end of Act 1, Tristan and Isolde drink a love potion, and, as Ford's narrator suggests, the rest of the opera focuses on their passion for each other. Ford's father, Franz Hueffer had founded the magazine *Musical World* to champion Wagner's work, "the Music of the Future". Ford's wife, Elsie, would sing from "Tristan and Isolde" (See Saunders, 20, 119.) Ford wrote on Wagner in his war-time propaganda book, *When Blood is Their Argument: An Analysis of Prussian Culture* (London: Hodder and Stoughton, 1915).

China tea (p.42): China tea had been introduced into London coffee-houses shortly before 1660. I have been unable to identify the "little measures on the tops of the new canisters".

loaf-cutter (p.45): "lady" is derived from the Old English "hlafdige". "Hlaf" is "loaf", "dige" means "knead" (compare with modern "dough")—so the kneader of bread rather then the cutter of bread.

though the skies fall (p.46): a reference to the Latin maxim *Fiat justitia, ruat caelum*. Conrad used the phrase in a letter to Marguerite Poradowska (March 1890), written shortly before he left for the Congo, and he alludes to it in the closing paragraphs of "Heart of Darkness": "The heavens do not fall for such a trifle. Would they have fallen I wonder, if I had rendered Kurtz that justice which was his due?"

four railways ... heaven knows how many mines (p.52): The text alludes to the late-Victorian period of financial speculation that included "railway mania" (speculation on railway building) and later various financial scandals relating to gold and diamond mines. For a fuller account of this, see Robert Hampson, *Conrad's Secrets* (Basingstoke: Palgrave, 2012).

Herb Oblivion (p.55): He is perhaps referring to the herb "moly", which appears in Book 10 of Homer's *Odyssey*. However, Hermes gives this herb to Odysseus to protect him from Circe's magic—not to produce forgetfulness, but rather to save him from self-forgetting. There is perhaps a confusion with the Lethe, one of the five rivers of Hades: those who drank from it experienced complete forgetfulness.

chloral (p.60): i.e. chloral hydrate. After the publication of an account of its sedative properties in 1869, chloral hydrate was widely used in the Victorian period (and after). It was used as a cure for insomnia, but it was also used recreationally. Ford's uncle, Dante Gabriel Rossetti (1830-82) was a regular user of chloral.

our way very strait (p.61): Compare Matthew 7:14: "Because strait is the gate, and narrow is the way, which leadeth unto life, and few there be that find it".

Eurydice (p.64): In Greek mythology, Eurydice was a wood nymph or one of the daughters of Apollo, who became the wife of Orpheus. When she died, he travelled to the underworld to bring her back. He was allowed to do so on the condition that he walk in front of her and not look back. But he looked back and lost her. The myth was the subject of a number of operas including Monteverdi's *L'Orfeo* (1607) and Gluck's *Orfeo ed Euridice* (1762).

thumb up or down (p.69): The phrase (and gesture) derives from popular ideas about gladiatorial combats in classical Rome, where the fate of a defeated fighter was determined by gestures from the crowd. Jean-Léon Gérôme's painting *"Pollice Verso"* (1872), in which the crowd have their thumbs down, is credited as the source of the popular understanding of the gesture. However, classical texts do not unambiguously support the notion that thumbs up meant survival and thumbs down death: it has been argued that the gestures had the opposite meaning.

THE NATURE OF A CRIME
AN AFTERWORD
By Robert Hampson

"THE NATURE OF A CRIME" was the third of three collaborations between Joseph Conrad and Ford Madox Ford. The first, *Romance*, an attempt at a Stevensonian adventure story set in the Caribbean of the 1820s, was a genuine collaboration, written between the autumn of 1898 and the spring of 1902. At the beginning of September 1898, Conrad and his wife Jessie went to stay with the Garnetts at Limpsfield in Surrey. There they met Ford Hueffer (as he was then called) and his wife Elsie, who had taken a cottage nearby in order to live "the simple life". Ford was 24 years old, but he had already published three fairy tales for children, a volume of poetry, a biography of his grandfather Ford Madox Brown, and a novel *The Shifting of the Fire*. Conrad was almost 41 and had published *Almayer's Folly*, *An Outcast of the Islands*, *Tales of Unrest* and *The Nigger of the "Narcissus"*—and he was struggling with *The Rescue*, the third of his trilogy of novels about Tom Lingard. Ford was working on a novel of Kentish smugglers and Caribbean pirates—at that point called "Seraphina"—which he seems to have read to Conrad at

Conrad's home, Pent Farm, shortly after they met. Conrad's criticisms of the novel led to the decision to work together on re-writing it, while each also pursued their own separate projects. In Conrad's case, these included *Lord Jim* (1900) and "Heart of Darkness" (1900). For Ford, it meant his history-book *The Cinque Ports* (1900) and a novel *The Benefactor* (1905). "Seraphina" was re-written and published as *Romance: A Novel* in 1903.

The second work, *The Inheritors*, was actually the first fruit of the collaboration to be published: Ford began writing the novel in the summer of 1899 during a pause in his work on *Romance*, and it was published in 1901. *The Inheritors* was Ford's version of "Heart of Darkness", which was at that time being serialized in *Blackwood's Magazine*. Conrad's powerful narrative based on his experiences in the Belgian Congo was re-written by Ford as an odd hybrid of political satire, futuristic fantasy and *roman à clef*. As this suggests, *The Inheritors* was largely Ford's work with minimal contributions from Conrad: his main task seems to have been quality control, making Ford re-write the chapters over and over again. Conrad wrote to Edward Garnett (26 March 1910), when he heard that Heinemann had accepted the novel for publication, describing the collaboration: "I set myself to look upon the thing as a sort of skit upon the political novel ... And poor H was in dead earnest!"[i] He goes on to joke about how hard Ford worked: "There is not a chapter I haven't made him write twice—most of them three times over".[ii] When it was published, *The Inheritors* met with mixed reviews: a number of reviewers found it irritating or puzzling.[iii] The reviewer in the *Manchester Guardian* (10 July, 1901), however, described it as a "curious and entertaining book" and praised the authors as "exceedingly adroit in their half revelations".[iv] The reviewer in the *Daily Telegraph* (19 July 1901) thought that "Mr Conrad and Mr Hueffer collaborate to good purpose".[v] The reviewer in the *Daily News* (24 July 1901), after a perceptive analysis of the narrative, recommended the novel as "a book that should be read".[vi] One reviewer was particularly perspicacious about the nature of the collaboration: "perhaps we shall not be far wrong if we take it that the younger author contributes the central idea, the plot, and general situation, and first works out the various scenes in the rough, and that the elder man, bringing his experience of life and insight to bear, by a series of slight touches, recasting and deletions, gives the whole book that style, intention and atmosphere which the public has already seized in his former works as defining his judgement of life".[vii]

"The Nature of a Crime" again seems to have been almost entirely Ford's work. Conrad's role seems to have been limited to verbal comments and suggestions, when Ford read the manuscript to him—although Ford claimed that part of Chapter 1 was written by Conrad. The story was written in Winchelsea in May 1906, while Conrad was working there on *The Secret Agent*, and was published three years later in Ford's literary magazine, the *English Review*, under the pseudonym "Baron Ignatz von Aschendrof".[viii] The story re-appeared nearly twenty years later, when Ford asked Conrad if he might re-print it in the first two numbers of his new journal, the *transatlantic review*.[ix] It was at this point that each of the collaborators wrote the prefaces and Ford wrote his analysis of their collaboration on *Romance*. The story first appeared in book form (with the prefaces and an appendix which re-prints Ford's description of the collaboration with Conrad on *Romance*) shortly after Conrad's death in September 1924. Its appearance in book form after Conrad's death places it alongside Ford's posthumous memoir of Conrad, *Joseph Conrad: A Personal Remembrance* (1924), and his editing of Conrad's abandoned early novel *The Sisters* (1928). These can either be seen as acts of homage to the memory of an old friend or as an attempt to capitalise on that earlier friendship. Certainly many of the contemporary reviews related the appearance of "The Nature of a Crime" to Conrad's death and the cultural value of Conrad's name. Thus W. L. Courtney, in the *Daily Telegraph*, began his review by observing that the work "has been restored from oblivion mainly because every scrap that bears the name of Conrad is precious to our eyes".[x] Courtney's statement is nicely poised on the cultural and material value of this republication. Other reviews, however, less delicately questioned whether the novella should have been "exhumed".[xi] This recalls Conrad's own doubts, when Ford proposed republishing the story: "If you think it advisable to dig up this affair, well, I don't see how I can object".[xii]

Whatever the nature and extent of Conrad's involvement in the writing of the story, "The Nature of a Crime" was written during the period of close interaction between Conrad and Ford, the decade that began with that meeting in 1898. In his memoir, *Return to Yesterday*, Ford recalls that he had, "much earlier, written about half a long short story having the same subject" and claims that the story "was one my grandfather used to tell about one of his wealthy Greek art patrons who, imagining himself to be ruined, wrote a letter to his mistress to the effect that he was going to commit suicide rather than be detected in a fraudulent bankruptcy and then found that the bankruptcy could be avoided".[xiii] In *A Personal Record* (1912), Conrad included his own family experience of swindling: he tells the story of his maternal great-grandmother, who, widowed at an early age "and left very well-off, married again a man of great charm and of an amiable disposition but without a penny" (APR, 49). This amiable man set about systematically depriving his stepsons of their inheritance "by buying and selling land in his own name and investing capital in such a manner as to cover up the traces of real ownership" (APR, 50):

> The critical time came when the elder of the boys on attaining his majority in the year 1811 asked for the accounts and some part at least of the inheritance to begin life upon. It was then that the stepfather declared with calm finality that there were no accounts to render and no property to inherit.   (APR, 50)

Conrad dictated this story to Ford at the end of 1908, two years after "The Nature of a Crime", for publication in *The English Review*. Clearly financial swindles and undetected criminals were in the minds of both Ford and Conrad in this period.

Conrad, for example, was to go on to write *Chance*, where one strand of the narrative involves a financier, de Barral, who runs what we would now call a Ponzi scheme, whereby high interest is promised on investments, but the interest payments are made out of the capital of subsequent investors—until the moment when the bubble bursts. In *Chance*, de Barral's companies grow and proliferate through their reassuring names, through the power of advertising, and through promotion by the press. As I have shown elsewhere, the figure of de Barral derives in part from Conrad's own experiences—including losing his inheritance through investing in a South African gold mine—and in part from high profile cases around the turn of the nineteenth century (such as those of Whitacker Wright, who, in January 1904, committed suicide by taking cyanide, when he was found guilty of fraud, and Jabez Balfour, who fled to Argentina when his bank and network of companies collapsed in 1895).[xiv] These high profile swindles support Conrad's observation in his Preface about "the amount this fragment contains of the crudely materialistic atmosphere of the time" (p.7).[xv] Ford's interest in "the undetected criminal" in "The Nature of a Crime" chimes well with Conrad's conviction that the "true anarchist" was the millionaire.

"The Nature of a Crime" takes the form of an extended love letter or, rather, series of love letters written by the unnamed narrator to a married woman, who is visiting Rome, as Ford's wife was at the time, and a shorter letter written three days after he has posted the first batch. As Judd notes, "the tone and language of the book are Fordian".[xvi] Indeed, the opening sentence, as he observes, is "distinctively Fordian": "You are, I suppose, by now in Rome" (p.13). Not only does Ford re-use these opening lines in a poem, but this intimate address anticipates that of Dowell, the narrator of *The Good Soldier*. There Dowell imagines for himself an intimate situation and a sympathetic auditor:

> … I shall just imagine myself for a fortnight or so at one side of the fireplace of a country cottage, with a sympathetic soul opposite me. And I shall go on talking in a low voice while the sea sounds in the distance …[xvii]

However, in *The Nature of a Crime*, the auditor is not imaginary: she is the wife of a friend. But one of the questions that hovers over the letters is to what extent the character of the addressee is actually an imaginative construct of the writer's. He distinguishes early on between "my You" and "the you that every other man sees", but this claim of special intimacy rebounds upon him to suggest the possibility that "my You" is actually a delusion. Thus, he claims a sympathetic understanding between them, but he also reveals that "in all the years we have known each other—seven years, three months and two days—I have never had so long as ten hours in which I might talk to you" (p.20).

The first sequence of letters moves forward in time over a period of seven days. The writer's original intention is that, by the time the letter is delivered, he will have committed suicide and the letter will be read after his death. This gives him the freedom to confess—his love for the addressee, his crime, and even "the great secret": "every time I left your presence, it was with the desire, the necessity to forget you" (p.18). It was this desire to forget her, he claims, that led him to gambling "first with my own money and then with money that was not mine" (p.19). He breaks off writing, at first, because it grows late and he gets tired, but then, in subsequent letters, because he has settled into a habit of nocturnal letter-writing. However, because the writing process is spread over a period of time, the circumstances in which he is writing also change. Thus each letter looks backwards (if only to the events of the evening or the day before), but also forwards into a future that is constantly changing, constantly being revised. This complex chronology is one of the most interesting technical features of the work. At the start, the writer is intending a final avowal of his love before he commits suicide: he has received a letter, which has created the crisis, and he expects his crime to be revealed and his arrest to follow the next morning. As far as he is concerned, he is writing to her from beyond the grave, and this perspective heightens his responses and frees his confession. Subsequent letters, after he fails to be arrested, are written in response to further changes in his circumstances or to new expectations of particular future events. His encounter with Edward Burden's fiancée, for example, the day after his first letter, leads him to propose to his addressee the following evening: "If you desire me to live on, I will live on" (p.30), a radical revisioning of his possible future.

"The Nature of a Crime" is, as an early reviewer suggested, the study of a man at a crisis in his life.[xviii] The components of the novella are the relationship between the narrator and the woman he addresses—or, more accurately, the various confessions he makes to his version of the addressee—and the story he tells of his role as the sole trustee of the Burden Estate. The first, to use the sub-title of *The Good Soldier*, is "a tale of passion"; the second is the story of a crime. The narrative traces the shifting relations between the two. At the same time, we are reminded (towards the close of the letters) that the narrator is a successful business man: he has "originated four railways in tropical climates and one in the West of England: and opened up heaven knows how many mines of one kind or another" (p.52). In the case of Edward Ashburnham, in *The Good Soldier*, Ford is determined to make it clear that the emotional crisis which provides his "affair" is only a small fraction of the protagonist's existence.

Here, however, his protagonist's working life has been his escape from his love for his friend's wife, and the "gambling" he has undertaken goes beyond his defrauding of the Burden Estate into speculations of a different kind: he has taken part in the railway mania of the Victorian period, when fortunes were gained and lost on speculative investments in railways at home and abroad, and in the later craze for speculations in gold and diamond mines. The narrator's "gambling", and his swindling of the Burden Estate, needs to be seen as part of this larger context. It is no accident that the writer amuses himself by thinking about the shock Edward Burden would receive from the revelation of his actions: "It will certainly shake his belief in all accepted reputations—for he will look on the faces of many men each 'as solid as the Bank of England,' and he will think: 'I wonder if you are like ————'" (pp.62-3).

Gambling is a recurrent motif in the novel. In his first letter, the writer makes a "pact with Providence", whereby the non-appearance or re-appearance of a mouse will be read, respectively, as a sign of "an eternal life or the herald of nothingness" (p.23). In his meditation on the "debauchery" of Edward's "case of conscience", Edward's involvement with the young woman he has "kept" for the last two years is also presented as a gamble: "he was actually staking his all upon the chance that he could both take what he desired and afterwards reconcile it with his conscience to make a good match" (pp.39-40). Similarly, in his meditation on women's choice between respectable marriage and "dangerous men", the writer presents women as gamblers, staking "their sentimental lives" on the game. Gambling re-appears as a motif in Ford's great war-novel, *Parade's End*. Sylvia in the smoking-lounge of the hotel near the Front tries to make a pact with the dead Father Consett: she offers to "leave off torturing Christopher" and "go into retreat ... for the rest of my life" if "when she raised her eyes and really looked round the room she saw in it one man that looked presentable".[xix] Her husband, Tietjens, similarly thinks of making "a pact with Destiny": "willingly, to pass thirty months in the frozen circle of hell, for the chance of thirty seconds in which to tell Valentine Wannop what he had answered back ... to Destiny!".[xx] In the case of "The Nature of a Crime", gambling is integral: it is not only the content of the writer's confession, it also becomes progressively the nature of that confession itself, as the writer leaves his future in the hands of the woman to whom he has confessed. The possibility that he has been deluded about their intimacy adds another dimension to this gamble.

Ford, then, can be seen as the author of high-concept fantasy. As Richard Curle noted in his early review, "The Nature of a Crime" interweaves three strands: a man who has loved his friend's wife without ever declaring himself; who robs a client for excitement to compensate for his undeclared and unrequited love; who, at the same time, self-defeatingly has dedicated himself to saving the woman's husband from his drug-addiction.[xxi] The novella brings together love and economics—or, rather, unrequited love and fraud—like Conrad's novel *Chance* or Ford's *The Good Soldier*. But the complicating elements here are not just the saving of the husband, but also the doubt instilled in the reader whether the woman who is the object of his love shares his feelings. His largest gamble, in the end, is the declaration of his feelings to this woman, although he also tries to put pressure on her by making her responsible for his subsequent honesty or fraudulence.

[i] Joseph Conrad to Edward Garnett, 26 March 1900, Frederick R. Karl & Laurence Davies (eds), *The Collected Letters of Joseph Conrad,* vol. 2 (Cambridge: Cambridge University Press, 1986), 256-7.

[ii] Ibid. 257.

[iii] The reviewer in the *Daily Chronicle* (11 July 1901), for example, describes how s/he "closed the covers with disappointment, not to say vexation", and expresses particular "irritation at that asthmatic dialogue". See Allan H. Simmons (ed.), *Contemporary Reviews*, vol.1 (Cambridge: Cambridge University Press, 2012), 353-4.

[iv] *Contemporary Reviews*, 1.352-3.

[v] *Contemporary Reviews*, 1.355-7.

[vi] *Contemporary Reviews*, 1.357-8.

[vii] *The Academy* (20 July 1901), 43; *Contemporary Reviews*, 1.357.

[viii] The pseudonym was derived from the name of one of Ford's ancestors, Anton Wilhelm Aschendorff.

[ix] The story appeared in *transatlantic review*, January and February 1924.

[x] W. L. Courtney, *The Daily Telegraph* (26 September 1924), 15; reprinted in Mary Burgoyne and Katherine Isobel Baxter (eds), *Contemporary Reviews*, vol. 4 (Cambridge: Cambridge University Press, 2012), 388-91, 388.

[xi] John Franklin, *The New Statesman* (25 October 1924), 82; *Contemporary Reviews*, 4.401. See particularly Thomas Moult, "The Conrad-Huffer Pact", *The Bookman*, November 1924, 4.117-8. Moult begins by observing that "All is grist these days to the devout Conradian's mill", and then casts doubt on Conrad's motives in letting such a "tentative fragment" be re-published by noting that this decision was made at "a moment when inflated prices were being offered for Conrad's work" (*Contemporary Reviews*, 4.401-2). North American reviewers were particularly scathing about the price being asked by Doubleday for such a slight volume: Allan Nevins, for example, wittily observed that "The title has no reference to the fact that Doubleday, Page charge $2.50 for its 108 pages". See *The Sun* (New York), 27 September 1924, 6; *Contemporary Reviews*, 4. 406.

[xii] Conrad to Ford , 10 November 1923, Laurence Davies & Gene M. Moore (eds), *The Collected Letters of Joseph Conrad*, vol. 8 (Cambridge: Cambridge University Press, 2008), 216

[xiii] Ford Madox Ford, *Return to Yesterday* (London: Victor Gollancz, 1931), 199. Again Ford's truth-telling is confirmed by the existence of an early sketch of the story, with the title "The Old Story", as an unpublished typescript in the Kroch Library, Cornell University.

[xiv] See Robert Hampson, *Conrad's Secrets* (London: Palgrave Macmillan, 2012), Chapter 4.

[xv] The reviewer in the *Freeman's Journal* (13 December 1924) noted that the "central situation" of the novella "is a close parallel to that of Mr Granville Barker's 'The Voysey Inheritance'", *Contemporary Reviews*, 416.

[xvi] Alan Judd, *Ford Madox Ford* (London: Flamingo, 1991), 71.

[xvii] Ford Madox Ford. *The Good Soldier* (1915; New York: Vintage Books, 1955), 12.

xviii "Conrad and Collaborator", *Birmingham Post* (7 October 1924), 6; *Contemporary Reviews*, 396-7, 397.

xix Ford Madox Ford, *Parade's End* (Harmondsworth: Penguin, 1982), 414.

xx *Parade's End*, 339.

xxi Richard Curle, "Conrad and Hueffer: Early Joint Work with New Prefaces", *Daily Mail* (30 September 1924), 13; *Contemporary Reviews*, 393.

FURTHER READING

Biography:

Alan Judd, *Ford Madox Ford* , London: Flamingo, 1990.

Max Saunders, *Ford Madox Ford: A Dual Life*, Oxford: Oxford University Press, 1996.

Criticism:

Dennis Brown and Jenny Plastow (eds), *Ford Madox Ford and Englishness*, Amsterdam: Rodopi, 2006.

Laura Colombino (ed.), *Ford Madox Ford and Visual Culture*, Amsterdam: Rodopi, 2009.

Vita Fortunati and Elena Lamberti (eds), *Ford Madox Ford and "The Republic of Letters"*, Bologna: CLUEB, 2002.

AN AFTERWORD

Andrzej Gasiorek and Daniel Moore (eds), *Ford Madox Ford: Literary Networks and Cultural Transformations*, Amsterdam: Rodopi, 2008.
Robert Hampson and Tony Davenport (eds), *Ford Madox Ford: A Reappraisal*, Amsterdam: Rodopi, 2002.

Robert Hampson and Max Saunders (eds), *Ford Madox Ford's Modernity*, Amsterdam: Rodopi, 2003.

Jason Harding (ed.), *Ford Madox Ford: Modernist Magazines and Editing*, Amsterdam, Rodopi, 2010.

Sara Haslam (ed.), *Ford Madox Ford and the City*, Amsterdam: Rodopi, 2005.

Dominique Lemarchal and Claire Davison-Pégon (eds), *Ford Madox Ford, France and Provence*, Amsterdam: Rodopi, 2011.

Frank MacShane, *The Life and Work of Ford Madox Ford*, New York: Horizon Press, 1966.

Paul Skinner (ed), *Ford Madox Ford's Literary Contacts*, Amsterdam: Rodopi, 2007.

Joseph Wiesenfarth (ed.), *History and Representation in Ford Madox Ford's Writings*, Amsterdam: Rodopi, 2004.

Ford Madox Ford Society:
www.open.ac.uk/Arts/fordmadoxford-society

Also published by ReScript Books...

Dracula's Precursors:
The Mysterious Stranger
& other stories

An evocative setting in the Carpathian Mountains; an enigmatic aristocrat living alone in a vast ruin who seems to have dominion over wolves; a vampire who retreats to a coffin in a ruined crypt during the daytime and can only be vanquished by staking; a beautiful young woman in peril.... No, this isn't *Dracula*, but a story written some 70 years before Bram Stoker appropriated these elements for his classic novel.

"The Mysterious Stranger" was published anonymously in German in 1823 and translated into English soon after, during a time of enthusiasm for all things Gothic and Romantic.

Long out of print, it is presented here along with two other less familiar early vampire tales: **"The Last Lords of Gardonal"** (1867) by William Gilbert, the father of the famous D'Oyly Carte librettist, and Mary Cholmondeley's 1890 chiller, **"Let Loose"**.

David Annwn's informative introduction sets the context.

ReScript Books, 2011, ISBN 978-1-874400-49-3, UK price £9.00

The Ivory Gate:
Later Poems & Fragments
Thomas Lovell Beddoes

THOMAS LOVELL BEDDOES (1803-1849) was an English poet and dramatist whose early play *The Brides' Tragedy* was highly praised. He studied medicine at the Universities of Göttingen and Würzburg, where his involvement in radical politics led to his deportation. He spent the rest of his life in Switzerland and Germany, continuing to write but showing only occasional and fleeting interest in publication. His celebrated drama *Death's Jest-Book* and his *Collected Poems* were published posthumously.

This volume, edited and with an introduction by Alan Halsey, makes available separately for the first time the surviving text and fragments of Beddoes' unfinished work *The Ivory Gate*, together with a collection of his later poetry.

ReScript Books, 2011, ISBN 978-1-874400-50-9, UK price £9.00